# PERSONA
# NON GRATA

# PRAISE FOR *PERSONA NON GRATA*

"Stirling's tale of a modern knight on a quest weaves intrigue, drama, and faith into a page-turning narrative that's all-too topical to the modern political landscape. In the vein of both Indiana Jones and Jack Ryan, Paladin Smith is a teacher-wanderer called to put aside his past and rescue an old friend from a land on a countdown to revolution. With no backup, no weapons, Paladin must stand alone against the machinations of wicked men and princes to snatch the innocent from the flames of the coming war. But if time and toll have taught Paladin Smith anything, it's that sometimes the only way forward is through."

—**MATTHEW CARSON**, author of *The Backwards Mask*
and the Black Rook-7 series

"Stirling has an enjoyable, easy-reading style. *Persona Non Grata* plops the reader in the front seat of an exhilarating ride through the landscape of international diplomacy. Corruption, intrigue, and high-level politics form the blockades that the hero, Paladin Smith, must deal with in order to save a lost friend, preserve a free nation, and give us a modern-day parable where all things are possible with the Lord."

—**RANDY LINDSAY**, author of *End's Beginning: The Gathering*

"Combine James Bond and Parley P. Pratt into one character and you've got Paladin Smith, the hero of *Persona Non Grata*. This latest work by Stephen J. Stirling will thrill you, enthrall you, and entertain you as you follow an unlikely hero through the shark-infested waters of international politics on an exciting journey that feels like it's ripped from today's headlines. I found myself cheering for an underdog with unseen resources, and holding my breath as the fate of a people rested on his humble shoulders."

—**BROCK BOOHER**, author of *Healing Stone*

"Stephen J. Stirling's debut novel, *Persona Non Grata*, follows the story of a young and adventurous American teacher, Paladin Smith, as he seeks to rescue a former pupil from an increasingly volatile situation in Crimea. Full of suspense and political intrigue, this book's message is two-fold: first, that we should trust God's guiding Hand in our lives; and second, that loyalty to liberty is what counts—messages that surely need repeating again and again in our world today."

—**D. M. ANDREWS**, author of *The Serpent in the Glass*

"*Persona Non Grata* brings the adventure of Indiana Jones to Mormon literature."

—**RYAN RAPIER**, author of *The Reluctant Blogger*

# PERSONA
# NON GRATA

## STEPHEN J. STIRLING

BONNEVILLE BOOKS
AN IMPRINT OF CEDAR FORT, INC.
SPRINGVILLE, UTAH

This is a work of fiction. The characters, names, incidents, places, and dialogue are products of the author's imagination and are not to be construed as real. The opinions and views expressed herein belong solely to the author and do not necessarily represent the opinions or views of Cedar Fort, Inc. Permission for the use of sources, graphics, and photos is also solely the responsibility of the author.

ISBN 13: 978-1-4621-1450-4

Published by Bonneville Books, an imprint of Cedar Fort, Inc.
2373 W. 700 S., Springville, UT 84663
Distributed by Cedar Fort, Inc., www.cedarfort.com

LIBRARY OF CONGRESS CATALOGING-IN-PUBLICATION DATA

Stirling, Stephen J., 1953-
Persona non grata / Stephen J. Stirling.
    pages cm
  ISBN 978-1-4621-1450-4 (pbk. : alk. paper)
  1. High school teachers--Fiction. 2. Crimea (Ukraine)--Fiction. 3. Americans--Ukraine--Fiction. 4. Corruption--Ukraine--Fiction. 5. Political fiction. I. Title.
  PS3619.T577P47 2014
  813'.6--dc23
                                    2014006161

Cover design by Kristen Reeves
Cover design © 2014 by Lyle Mortimer
Edited and typeset by Melissa J. Caldwell

Printed in the United States of America

10 9 8 7 6 5 4 3 2 1

*To the best friends a man could have—*
*a good wife and five loving children.*

# CONTENTS

# Contents

# Author's Note on Crimea

**In the autumn of 2008,** I began to write an action adventure novel which I christened *Persona Non Grata*. The story had a simple message: God is still interested in the affairs of men and continues to guide our lives. As a backdrop for that ponderous thesis, I needed a stage on which my players could perform. That theater turned out to be Crimea—a nation which I created out of whole cloth.

Located east of the Crimean Peninsula and north of Georgia and Azerbaijan, my "fictional" Crimea is a constitutional monarchy nestled between the Black and Caspian Seas in what is today 120,000 square miles of southern Russia. It's actually quite small as fictitious countries go. I didn't think Vladimir Putin would mind my borrowing it. (I had no idea how sensitive and aggressive he was about Russian real estate.)

As this novel was about to go to press, a banner headline splashed across the newspapers of the world: "Russia Invades Crimea." Of course, it wasn't exactly the same Crimea which I had manufactured for this novel. But a few of the similarities were staggering.

With that in mind, let me say a word regarding the real Crimea and her actual national status. An "autonomous republic," Crimea has been recognized as part of the "independent nation of Ukraine" since the breakup of the Soviet Union. Of course, we're beginning to discover that Vladimir Putin, in his own way, doesn't believe the Soviet Union ever broke up. But that is another issue.

Written five years ago, this novel does not pretend to reflect the intricate elements of the current Crimean crisis. However, true to the narrative of *Persona Non Grata*, the Red armies of 2014 did invade Crimea, and did so at the request of the republic's ambitious "would-be" rulers, in an occupation that took the world by relative surprise. And that world was prepared to do little more than look on in helpless impotence.

The scenario in *Persona Non Grata* presents the story of a common man who steps into this maelstrom to stand for what is right and to do uncommon things. It is one pleasant outcome of a real situation—all part of a complex world that is not so fictitious after all. One thing is certain: the current international situation in Eastern Europe is an ominous sign of the perilous times in which we live. And there will be more to come.

# Prologue

THE AMERICAN STOOD erect on the forward deck of the Russian yacht. Cloaked in the shadows of the night, he stared silently over the dark expanse of the Black Sea. Impeccably attired in a dinner tuxedo, he wore the confident expression of a man in control of his world—with the cynical smile of one who intended to retain that control at any cost. He laughed softly to himself and gripped the railing. Under his feet the yacht churned at leisure through the water as waves lapped against the bow. Breathing deeply of the Crimean air, he felt himself at one with the luxury craft—the perfect blend of elegance, power, and heartless drive.

He shifted his weight ever so slightly as the yacht rocked on the surface of the water. Like himself, the ship had no sympathies or loyalties. Built of cold steel and lifeless wood, it was designed for self-indulgence, pleasure, and the display of ambitious superiority. And anything that lay in its course beyond the bow would be crushed and sent sinking to the bottom of the sea. He smiled again and peered contemptuously into the black distance, defiant of anything that would come into his path.

Behind him a steward cleared his throat. "Sir, the secretary will see you now."

The American turned emotionlessly and walked past the steward to the staterooms. He knew his way to the cabin occupied by the Russian official who waited for him. He opened the door and entered without knocking.

A distinguished, gray-haired Russian stood behind a large desk. He was only slightly surprised at the insolent air of his American guest. "Mr. Ambassador," he greeted him without smiling. "Sit down, please. I apologize for not welcoming you sooner. I've been on the telephone with our patron."

The ambassador nodded and sat in a cushioned chair. "Please relay my compliments to your president. His yacht is magnificent. I've been admiring the horizon."

"Indeed?" The man behind the desk cocked an eyebrow. "What horizon can you possibly appreciate at midnight?"

The guest smiled. "I've learned that the cover of darkness always provides a superior view, providing one knows precisely what lies in the waters ahead."

"You come to the point quickly," said the Russian, taking his seat. "That is, of course, the reason I am here—to verify that we *do* know what is just ahead. We venture into perilous 'international' waters."

The American leaned forward. "Mr. Secretary, our course is perfectly set. We know exactly where our vessel is going. Every detail of our voyage has been flawlessly arranged."

"As per our discussions, I am sure." The secretary shifted in his chair. "Your services and contacts have been invaluable. My president merely wants to make sure that there will be no interference from NATO or from the United States."

"Your president should know better," the visitor soothed. "He is well aware how the wind blows in America these days. There will be no intervention from the United States, the United Nations, or anyone else. In seven days the Russian Federation will be some two percent larger than it is today. And I will be some five hundred percent richer than I am today. But how uncouth! Who can put a price tag on patriotism or other noble aspirations of the heart?"

The Russian was stoic. "Setting aside the American sarcasm, my friend, Alexander Trotsky seeks a final assurance that we will encounter no unforeseen obstacles."

"You may give Alexander Trotsky my personal pledge," said the American as he casually lit a cigarette. "Every element in our little drama is in place, like the pieces of a brilliantly played game of chess. The checkmate is certain. There is no man on earth and no power in the universe that can stand in our way."

# 1

## Paladin Smith

THE SUN HAD just begun to brim over the California foothills, cast-
ing long shadows across the urban landscape. The orange morning light splashed onto the icy patches of grass to paint a dazzling
pattern of a million tiny prisms. It was a crisp morning for the first
day of school—at least in Santa Ana. It didn't usually get chilly
until late October. But the weather had been strange this year.

Paladin Smith stood on the stairs leading to his classroom,
silently absorbing the beauty of the morning. Within minutes the
frost would melt, the dawn would wane into day, and the moment
would be gone. He smiled, sighed, and sat on the wall that enclosed
the steps. He pulled one foot up comfortably atop the wall and
rested a forearm on his knee. He was in no hurry.

Paladin adjusted the wool scarf snugly around his neck as he
took a deep breath of the brisk morning air. He glanced at the stee-
ple of the church rising above the trees a block away. That's where
he had opened his day two hours ago, before the sun had begun
to stretch its fingers across the purple sky. For the past three years

he had greeted each day as Brother Smith, the seminary teacher, before crossing the street to become Mr. Smith, the history teacher.

And, of course, that made him unique.

For one thing, he was the only teacher on the high school faculty who wore a white shirt and a tie to class every day, amid a sea of T-shirts, Levi's, and sneakers. "Too much of a hassle to change each morning" was his standard explanation. But truth be known, Paladin was just comfortable these days with the missionary appearance, though he never quite cinched the tie up to his neck.

He was also comfortable with a short-cropped haircut, though his hair had seldom grown below his collar, even in his days on the road. And he'd never worn a beard.

Paladin did make one concession to individuality that became his trademark. The scarf. Getting up at 4:00 a.m. to teach seminary every morning was invigorating, but hard on his system in one respect. He was cold. Whether his metabolism was slow or he had molasses flowing in his veins, Paladin simply found it impossible to warm up on those early mornings—even in California. So he began wearing a scarf to seminary.

At first he'd take it off on arrival, but soon decided to leave it on through his lesson. Eventually, the scarf crossed the street with him to his high school classroom. And finally, it ended up hanging around his neck for the entire day in his air-conditioned building.

Of course, his fellow faculty members thought it was odd. But his students grew to recognize it as Mr. Smith's unique "freak flag"—the one quality about him that, surrounded by conventionality, indeed made him distinctive. He was at once a visual statement of conformity and rare rebellion. His projection was an element they hoped for in their future—the ability to function in the system while maintaining something of themselves—something intimate, original, and inviolate.

Paladin had no idea how long he had been sitting in this reverie.

He had only come outside for a moment—just to see the sunrise. Now the sun was several degrees in the sky, the dew was gone from the grass, and he became aware of students passing him on the concrete steps. "Hi, Mr. Smith." "Good morning, Mr. Smith." "Have a good summer, Mr. Smith?"

Snapping out of his own thoughts, Paladin hopped from the wall to join the teenagers climbing the stairs. He began answering their greetings in earnest. "Yes, it was a great summer. Too short though. What do you think, Trevor?"

"That's for sure, Mr. Smith. Did you go anywhere exciting?"

"Nah, you know the Smiths. We visit Tijuana. Maybe go camping once or twice. That's about all the thrills I can take."

He passed through the doors of the building as a finger tapped him on the shoulder. "Hey, Brother Smith. Long time, no see."

He turned and smiled at one of his seminary students. "Hi, Ashley. Didn't I just have a class with you two hours ago?"

"Yep." She laughed. "I just couldn't get enough."

At his classroom door, he stopped and turned as she filed past him. Then he stood at the threshold for a full minute or two, shaking hands with the rest of the students as they entered, a gesture that caught many of them off guard. One boy he didn't recognize paused briefly to look at his schedule. "Are you Mr. Smith—European History?"

"No," he said, grinning, "I'm Mr. Smith—World History. But you'll find there's not that much difference." The bell in the hallway rang. He glanced at it. "Come on in and find a seat."

—

The classroom was buzzing in a circus of conversations as Mr. Smith entered, closing the door behind him. He slowly approached the front of the room and leaned on the lectern in the corner. An apple—his lunch—was perched on top, along with his class roll pinched onto a clipboard. With a bland smile on his face, he waited there for a long minute, fiddling with the apple and observing his students—most of whom seemed unaware of him.

Three boys entered the room, clearly late, and sat by some friends. Another conversation began. Smith gradually straightened to his full height of five feet eight inches—not exactly, as he was well aware, a stature of commanding attention. The students continued to largely ignore him.

He cleared his throat at mid-volume. "I, uh—I'm not interrupting anyone, am I?" The student noise diminished slightly, but most of the classroom hum went on. This was, after all, the first day of school. He knew they were all pretty excited to see each other. But the real truth of the matter was that most of the students were just plain rude.

"Good to see you, Mr. Smith," said a student on the front row.

"Yes, isn't it though!" Paladin answered amiably. The chatter continued.

The class of thirty-two teenagers was pretty evenly divided between former students and students who had never seen Mr. Smith before. The initiated knew enough to settle down by now. That wasn't to suggest that they had any idea how he intended to bring order. No one ever knew what the history teacher would do from moment to moment. He was never that predictable. They simply knew from experience that he *would* do something. The others were oblivious to this reality and kept talking. After all, class hadn't really begun yet.

Smith casually strolled over to the side of the room and picked up a black baseball bat that was leaning against the wall. "My dear friends, I can tell you're excited to be here on this, the first day of class." Not much change. He smiled and hefted the bat in both hands. "This is a *Louisville Slugger,* thirty-two ounces of perfectly-balanced, crafted, polished maple."

Poising the bat vertically, he scanned it with admiration. His eyes rested on the logo and, below it, the monogram: *Presented to Paladin Smith—Midwest Baseball Challenge—2001.* He continued. "In the hands of someone who knows how to use it, this stick of lumber can send a baseball soaring four hundred feet over the garden wall." The bat arched down and he leaned on it like a cane. "It is a symbol not only of the national game but also of American society itself."

Paladin had their partial attention. But since they never really paid full attention in any other class, why should they here? With the bat still in hand, Smith walked to the opposite side of the room where a huge, beautifully decorated pot stood four feet from base to brim. "This is a vase, a reproduction from the Ming Dynasty, dating from approximately the fourteenth to the sixteenth centuries. It represents the greatest in art, culture, and technology that the world of the Orient had to offer that corner of the globe."

Mr. Smith glanced up. As he fully expected, his introduction to World History had left them indifferent. Less than half of them were even looking at him. "Okay. What do you suppose would be the result of the inevitable meeting of these two cultures?"

No answer. Smith smiled and took a deep breath. The students who knew him braced themselves.

"LET ME REPHRASE MY QUESTION!" Paladin suddenly raised his voice to a level that could be heard throughout the building. He strode to the front, center of the class. "LISTEN CAREFULLY," he shouted, hefting the bat again in both hands as he stepped deliberately over to the huge vase. "WHAT WOULD BE THE OUTCOME WHEN THE MODERN WESTERN WORLD EVENTUALLY CLASHED WITH THIS LESS-SOPHISTICATED ORIENTAL SOCIETY?"

He hadn't even finished the question before he settled into a perfect batters position a few feet from the vase. Without waiting an instant for the imaginary pitch, his face tightened, and he swung the bat toward the fences in one flawless and powerful motion. As he made contact the vase shattered into a thousand pieces, which showered around the room.

Mr. Smith stood amid the dust and wreckage, covered with shards of clay. Wide-eyed students were too stunned to speak. Even the veterans had never seen anything like it. He certainly had their attention. Conversations were frozen in mid air.

Paladin scanned the room. He smiled calmly and spoke evenly. "Now, who can answer my question?" He spotted one girl on the front row, her mouth hanging open with a cell phone still stuck to her face. "You," he said, pointing at her.

She slammed the phone onto her desk, hesitated briefly, and then stammered out a response. "I—forgot the question."

"That's okay," Smith answered patiently. "What happened when modern western civilization"—he held up the bat—"met the woefully unprepared, antiquated society of China?" As he finished he pointed with the bat to the shattered remnants of the Ming vase. Then he looked back to her encouragingly.

She spoke with timid uncertainty. "The Chinese got smashed?"

The class was still absolutely silent. Smith straightened to his full height. Cocking one eyebrow, he gave every indication of being extremely impressed. "Wow! That's very good. What's your name?"

"Velora," the girl answered blankly.

Smith hurried to his lectern, moved the apple aside, and picked up the clipboard. He scanned down the names. "Velora Sharp."

"Yes."

"Are you sure you haven't had this class before?" There were a few giggles around the room. A stern look from Mr. Smith let them know he was still not to be trifled with. They became silent immediately. "Well, that's a great answer, Velora. I think you're going to do very well in this class."

The girl half smiled and sat up a little straighter.

"As a matter of fact, I think you're all going to do well in this class—but only on a few conditions that we are going to have to make clear between us. I will respect you and you will respect me. You will listen and I will teach. You will not talk while I do so. And conversely when you make comments, I will listen to you. You will be on time to this class." Paladin craned his neck to catch the eyes of the three late boys, who smiled sheepishly.

Finally, he noted the cell phone still on Velora's desk on the front row. "And you will not use your cell phones in this class." As he spoke he moved toward her. "If you insist on using your cell phones, you will lose them."

He poised his bat over his head and took aim on the phone. In a quick, nervous gesture she swept the phone off her desk and into her purse. Smith lowered the bat and smiled. "I'm happy to see you know what that means."

Walking to the corner he leaned the bat against the blackboard and picked up a large stool, which he carried to the head of the classroom. Setting it down with one hand, he brushed the pottery shards from his jacket with the other, adjusted his scarf, and sat on the stool. "My name is Paladin Smith."

He watched one of the students trying to silently mouth the name.

"*Pal*-uh-din," he repeated. "Accent on the first syllable. A knight or hero. One of the twelve legendary champions from the court of Charlemagne. My closest friends call me Paladin. My friends who are students are welcome to call me Mr. Smith.

"I am thirty years old. I have been teaching at this high school for the past three years. Prior to my employment here I made a living persuading people to purchase things they didn't want with money they didn't have—in the world of advertising. But in that field I didn't find the people or subject matter nearly as interesting as I do here in your company. I have also been married for a little over three years. All in all, I've never been happier."

Paladin paused and pondered for a moment. "What more can I tell you about myself? Let's see . . . I spent two years hitchhiking and riding rails as a professional tramp, I survived a South

American revolution in Argentina, in high school I was a member of the Black Panthers, and I've been driven out of town by the Mafia at least once. Any questions?"

One girl in the middle of the class timidly raised her hand. He nodded at her. "How did a white Anglo-Saxon kid become a member of the Black Panthers?" she asked.

"That is an adventure I'll tell you about later," he said, smiling. "I never make anything up. I also spent a day this summer in a Mexican jail. But that's also another story."

A boy in the back leaned over to one of the repeat students and broke the dead silence in a whisper that he didn't intend for others to hear. "Is he for real?"

The veteran nodded his head, smirked, and replied under his breath. "Shh! You'd better believe it!"

Paladin leaned back on the stool, picked up and polished the apple on the lectern, and smiled. Lesson number one had already been a smashing success.

—

Mr. Smith stood at the door and shook hands with every student as they left the classroom. "See you, Josh. On time tomorrow, right? Margaret, nice to have you here. Good comment. Wait a minute. Brittany? I thought so. Thanks for being here. Jordan, right? Great looking hat. Could you take it off in class from now on? Thank you. Good insight today."

As they left they knew that he liked them. And instinctively they liked him. One by one he acknowledged each of them individually—and most of them by name—until the room was empty. He followed them a few steps and watched as they disappeared down the hallway, actually laughing to themselves about their harrowing first hour experience in World History.

That lesson had been a tightrope act without a net, and Paladin knew it. He couldn't perform that trick every hour—and not merely because he only had one Ming vase. That was the kind of story that had to spread from mouth-to-mouth. Reputation was a delicate thing. It had to be cultivated.

Second period was his free "prep" hour, so Paladin had about sixty-five minutes for that incident to carry like feathers on the wind to the waiting ears of his next class. He wouldn't clean up the clay pieces. If the students from first hour did their job, the shattered remnants of sixteenth century Chinese culture would be all the silent testimony he would need to promote discipline for the rest of the year.

Rubbing his hands together Paladin turned and quickly walked back into the classroom. He needed to consider what the coming third hour experience might be. But arriving at his door he halted abruptly.

There at the front of the room stood two men, obviously waiting for him. One of them was tall and dressed in a well-tailored suit and wing-tip shoes. His entire physique was sculpted, from his molded frame and his handsome, chiseled face to his perfectly combed hair. But in all his appearance, the man's most distinguishing feature was a manufactured, plastic smile that seemed ceremoniously attached to his face for occasions precisely such as this.

The second man was shorter and not as polished, but he was just as well dressed. Everything about him suggested deference to the taller version—an unspoken pride that borrowed itself entirely from the presence of man number one.

Paladin remained at the doorway and folded his arms. As he did so, both visitors looked up at him and the taller man cranked the practiced smile a notch higher. In his hands he held one of the larger shards of the broken Ming vase. "What did I tell you, Dennis?" He dropped the shard into the pile that had once been the vase, and it broke in two. "Didn't I tell you he was an incredible teacher?"

The smaller man responded on cue. "I've never seen anything like it, sir."

"We were listening just outside the rear door of your classroom," the taller man gestured to the back of the room. "The effect was magical. You have a golden touch when it comes to reaching the hearts of today's youth."

Only now did Paladin take a cautious step into the classroom. His face was still expressionless. "You know me," he said. "I've had the golden touch for years."

The dazzling smile vanished from the face of the taller man, but only for a moment. Instantaneously it reappeared as fresh as if new off the assembly line. He stepped forward to regain his balance and reached out his hand. "How are you, Smith? It's been a few years."

Paladin graciously accepted the handshake, but his smile was merely a polite one. "I'm doing well, Congressman Chase. And it's been seven years—seven years this Christmas."

There was another uncomfortable pause as their handshake slowed to a stop. The congressman released his grip and backed away half a step. "Well, so it has. So it has." A new smile reanimated him. "Let me introduce my administrative assistant, Dennis Keaton."

"Nice to meet you, Mr. Keaton."

"The pleasure's mine, Mr. Smith. I've heard a great deal."

Paladin looked at Chase. "What have you heard?"

"I mentioned to Keaton that you used to teach my niece in your seminary a few years ago."

"Seven years ago," Paladin clarified in a soft but crisp voice, "this Christmas."

"Well, yes," Chase stammered. "I didn't recall exactly when."

"I do," interrupted Paladin. He glanced at the congressman and moved toward his assistant. "Maybe I should tell this story since I remember more of the details." He cleared his throat. "You see, Mr. Keaton, I was a young, enthusiastic college graduate out looking for work in the great wide world. I had a few ideas of what I wanted to do, but I really loved to teach. That's why I was excited when I was asked to teach an early morning seminary class. Seminary, Mr. Keaton, is religious instruction that the Church of Jesus Christ of Latter-day Saints offers its teenagers every morning before school. Of course, there's no pay, but the perks are great. You teach the scriptures to the eager and alert youth of Zion each day at 5:00 a.m., and the Church reimburses you for gasoline."

Paladin gestured for Keaton to sit down as though the congressman were not there. He himself took a comfortable place on the stool in front of the assistant and continued. "Still, I loved it. I had twenty-one students in my class that first year. That was a pretty big early morning group, but we had a passable good time for a non-credit class meeting before dawn each day to study the New Testament.

"Now there was one girl in that class that was having a bad year. She was seventeen years old. Her parents had died in a car accident, and the court had awarded her to an aunt and uncle. All this had happened over the summer. Social counselors had persuaded the new foster parents to allow her to continue going to her own church and to seminary—though the couple really didn't think too highly of the Mormons."

"That's not necessarily true," broke in Chase defensively.

"Thank you for that detail, Congressman. I can see that the cobwebs are clearing." Paladin paused. "Now, what was that girl's name?"

Congressman Chase didn't flinch, but he didn't smile. "Victoria Grant."

Paladin took a deep sigh. "Victoria Grant," he repeated to himself and shook his head. "She was a great girl. I believe I dropped by your law office one day to discuss her situation. I even stopped by the house one evening when she'd been sick for a few days."

"I remember."

"That whole class was full of great teenagers. I liked to show up at their sporting events and activities. Wrestling matches, cross-country meets, baseball games. Of course, it kept me pretty busy.

Those kids sang in the choir, they marched in the band, and they played in the orchestra. I went to as much of that stuff as I could. The students loved it, and the parents appreciated it. In fact, only one parent took any exception to it at all. He thought I was showing an *undue interest*. Wasn't that the legal term?"

"Perhaps I should have ignored the fact that a young teacher seemed to be stalking my teenage niece?"

"I was there for *all* their activities, Mr. Chase. And I was hardly stalking her."

"You paid *a lot* of attention to her."

Paladin sighed. "'Nice game, Victoria. That's quite a fastball. Great concert, Victoria. I didn't know you were first violin. Just wanted to let you know I came, Victoria.' I can see how threatening that was," he said sarcastically.

"I had a responsibility as her uncle!"

"To do exactly what, Congressman? To 'protect' her from someone who paid attention to her? At a time when she needed just a little attention, from anybody?"

"She was in love with you, Smith," Chase burst out.

Paladin became stone serious in the silence. "No, Congressman. Victoria was in love with Jace Packard."

Recognition lit up Keaton's boyish face. "Jace Packard?" He turned to Chase. "Isn't that the son of Merlin Packard?"

Paladin smiled bitterly and glanced at Chase. "Still one of your biggest contributors, I'll bet."

Keaton deflected the barb. "Well, he *is* one of the wealthiest men in Southern California."

"Yes, I know," drawled Paladin. "We used to call his pampered son 'The Prince of Orange County.' He attended the high school here in town and took a liking to Victoria Grant. And, of course, she fell for him."

"What was wrong with that?" interjected Chase. "He was a nice kid."

"Whose father had nice money. Jace Packard was a spoiled, rich punk who thought his daddy's bank account entitled him to anything he wanted." He stopped to stare at the congressman. "Anything!"

Chase answered without hesitation. "He was just a teenage boy doing what teenagers do. You overreacted."

"He was also the son of your richest client." Paladin shook his head, "But *she* was your niece. And you were willing to sacrifice her to keep Merlin Packard happy."

Keaton cleared his throat to break the tension. "Jace Packard is in jail now, I think."

"He should have been in jail then," Paladin seethed. "He beat Victoria one night and tried to rape her."

Chase rolled his eyes. "The boy got a little carried away on a date."

"Tell that to Victoria, Chase, or to the doctor who examined her bruises. But that could be ignored. After all, it's money that funds law firms and runs political campaigns."

"He was just a hot-blooded kid," muttered Chase.

"And do you know who she called, Mr. Keaton, when she fought herself free of that 'hot-blooded kid' and hid from him in the city park? Not the police, not her uncle—me!"

"You blew that whole thing way out of proportion," accused the congressman.

Paladin released a single laugh. "True. Right after Jace Packard tried to pound my face out of proportion with a tire iron."

"The boy told the story differently," corrected Chase. "Like I said, you overreacted."

"Did I?"

"You broke his arm and jaw with a trash can lid."

"I do things like that when someone tries to kill me."

"No other motivation, Smith?"

Paladin paused for a breath. "I'm just lucky I got there when I did. *Victoria* was grateful. You should have been."

"Grateful!" Chase stood to his feet. "You became Jace Packard's instant replacement. You must have known that. Couldn't you see she had a crush on you, Smith?"

"Right! She was seventeen. I was twenty-four. Where was *that* going to go? It would have worn off by the senior prom."

Chase took a deep breath to regain his composure. "Listen, I just did what I felt I had to do."

"And what you and your rich client had to do was charge me with assault and threaten to sue the Church. The bishop was scared to death. I offered to resign. Salt Lake[1] would have asked me to leave anyway. I'm sure *that* was a disappointment to you, you miserable ambulance chaser. Because I know you'd much rather have sued." Paladin had to stop himself in his tirade. He sighed thoughtfully. "I left town under the weight of a restraining order, and I never saw Victoria Grant again."

The congressman cleared his throat to fill the uncomfortable quiet. "Well, it was a manful and wise decision. I always wanted to tell you so. That, and no hard feelings." He held out his hand.

Paladin stared at Chase's hand incredulously, then glanced at his aid and back at the congressman. "You make your *living* at this, huh? You pander yourself on America's citizens and foreign neighbors, you peddle that phony smile of yours to the highest bidder, and then you stab your constituents in the back like you did me—and finally return to the crime scene with a disingenuous handshake and a pitiful 'no hard feelings.'"

Chase lowered his hand gravely. "I'm sorry you feel that way."

"I had a dream to teach full-time seminary someday. That will never happen now. An accusation like yours follows a man. You took everything away from me." He shook his head thoughtfully. "I admit I was foolish and idealistic at the age of twenty-four. But the worst judgment I ever made was not to run as far away as

---

1. Salt Lake City is the world headquarters of The Church of Jesus Christ of Latter-day Saints.

fast as I could the moment I met you—and forget I ever knew Victoria Grant."

Chase gave a barely perceptible nod. "In that you could be right."

"Incidentally," Paladin stood from the stool and dusted his hands clean, "my judgment did improve over the years. When you decided to run for Congress, I returned to California just to vote for the other guy."

Paladin turned and walked toward the door. Passing his lectern he grabbed the apple off the top and tossed it over his shoulder. "Nice to see you again, Congressman. Grab yourself a poisoned apple on your way out. And by the way, no hard feelings."

Chase caught the apple in one hand. "That's not why I came back, Smith. I need something."

Paladin was already gone. His voice echoed from the hallway, "Well, you came to the wrong place."

"It's not really me," the congressman answered loudly. "It's Victoria Grant. She's in trouble."

There was a long pause. Congressman Chase waited. He glanced at Keaton and smiled, holding his mouth open. "Did you hear me, Paladin?"

Smith stepped back into the doorway. His frame, which had been stiff with anger, was suddenly limp and drained of energy. "What's all this about, Chase?"

"Sit down, Smith. Please." The congressman gestured to a desk on the front row. As if on cue, Keaton pulled the seat out and turned it toward the one Chase was settling into. Paladin warily approached the desk and sat down as Keaton sat behind him.

Chase continued. "We've allowed the pain of old wounds to blur our purpose. That's all water under the bridge. Like I said, I've come here looking for help. Help only you can give me."

Paladin gave him a sidelong glance. "You've done a lousy sales job so far. Tell me about Victoria."

"Do you have any idea what Victoria has been up to for the past few years?"

"I haven't a clue. I assumed she'd gotten married and started a life. Most of those kids have."

The congressman laughed under his breath. "No, not Victoria. She's too rebellious for that. Too much of a free spirit. It was all I could do to get her into that high-status Mormon college of yours.[2] And it was all I could do to keep them from throwing her out. Right, Keaton? She never was much for their code of conduct." He sparkled his politician's grin. "Never underestimate the power of influence and position—even at 'The Lord's University.'" He chuckled.

Paladin was running out of patience. "We were talking about Victoria, not you."

"Yes," the congressman continued, "and we still are actually. After graduating with a degree in government science, Victoria used my influence to secure an introduction to a high-ranking American officer in our Ukrainian Consulate—Ian Keller. That was two years ago. Last January Keller was appointed ambassador to Crimea. Victoria moved up with him as an embassy assistant— an intern if you will. Works very closely with him."

"An intern! And *that* didn't bother you? Where's this Crimea?"

"Crimea is one of those little countries that spun off from the Soviet Union a few years back. Do you have that file, Keaton?"

Instantly a clean manila folder was placed on the desk in front of Paladin. "There you are, Mr. Smith," said Keaton. "Everything you need to know."

He glanced up at Keaton, then at Chase. "Why do I need to know anything?"

"Just look through the material," coaxed Chase. "We'll talk as you do."

---

2. Brigham Young University, or BYU, is owned and operated by The Church of Jesus Christ of Latter-day Saints. It is the largest religious university in America.

Paladin opened the folder. The first page was a map on State Department stationery. It was the shaded outline of the nation labeled "Crimea" nestled between the Black Sea and the Caspian Sea, just north of Georgia and Azurbaijan. He leafed through several pages of documents on the nation's constitutional monarchy, military structure, and political situation—much of it classified data.

Then he came to an 8 x 10 photograph of a man—a handsome and refined man, dressed in a tuxedo, somewhere in his forties, holding up a wine glass. He was obviously hosting some official function.

He wore a smile on his face, but the smile was an instant contrast to the constant smile on the face of Congressman Chase. Paladin unconsciously glanced up to compare the two and considered again. It was disconcerting. Suddenly Chase's grin was something comical—something not to be taken seriously. The smile on this man's face was different. It hid a multitude of deceptions. This smile was dangerous.

"Ian Keller," Chase's voice broke the silence. "The American ambassador to Crimea."

Paladin tore his eyes from the photograph and looked straight at Chase. "Why does the United States government employ men like that?"

The congressman was unapologetic. "Don't be naïve, Smith. We need people like that. Keller knows how to howl with the pack. He's useful."

Paladin turned to a second photograph of Keller. This photo showed him, again in formal attire at some embassy affair, dancing with a young woman. Even in the photograph Keller oozed with charm. But Paladin's attention was quickly drawn from Keller to the young woman. He looked at her more closely. She was also dressed formally, in an evening gown for the state function. Keller's hand around her waistline accented a trim figure.

However, her face was the focus of the picture. Her auburn hair, styled up for the event, gave full view of a perfect complexion, easy smile, and sparkling eyes. Her beauty seemed to complement

Keller's masculine charm. There again, in one glance, there was a contrast—something still basically innocent beside something intrinsically vile.

Paladin creased his brow almost painfully and looked up at Chase without moving his head.

"She's grown up a little," observed the congressman without expression. "But you can still recognize her after all these years."

"Seven years," whispered Paladin, staring at the photograph, "this Christmas." He finally broke the spell and turned the photo facedown. "She always dreamed of government work and seeing the world, even in high school. Looks like she got what she wanted."

"Perhaps more than she bargained for," commented Chase. "Look at the next picture."

Turning over the photo, Paladin found himself staring at the portrait of a king in full regalia, perfectly posed for a public relations shot. As he studied the face of the king, he saw the same kind of self-importance he recognized in Chase. But Chase at least knew how to conceal it. This man made no pretensions at false humility and obviously saw no need to. Paladin looked up at Chase.

"Pyotr Vasiliyevich, prince of Crimea. Styles himself 'Peter the Great.'" The congressman laughed to himself. "In committee we refer to him as 'Peter the Mediocre.'"

"Hmm," noted Paladin, more amused by the man than the joke. "He's got a crown, a scepter, and everything." Still there was an intensity about the prince that was not to be taken lightly. This was a tyrant in waiting. He was no joking matter at all. Paladin wondered if the congressman recognized it.

"Well, his position is merely titular in a constitutional monarchy," clarified Chase. "He really has no political power."

Paladin shook his head. "Maybe not. But he *wants* it."

"Very observant, Smith. Now take a look at the next photo."

The next photograph was a picture of the prince in formal wear at some kind of a royal function, eating dinner. Beside him on his right, looking radiant, sat Victoria Grant. "Victoria always had a knack for making friends," observed Paladin.

"The prince is actually quite taken with her."

"And why shouldn't he be? She looks like a princess." Paladin dropped the photo. "So, what more can you ask for—success, romance, dreams come true. It's all like a modern fairy tale."

"You know as well as I do, Paladin, that Victoria is in over her head here."

"Who's to say that?" argued Paladin, fighting his natural instincts. "The truth is, it's none of my business any more than it is yours. She's an adult now, Chase. Anyway, I still don't see what any of this has to do with me."

"Listen, Smith," Chase confided. "Crimea is a dangerous place right now. The civil unrest is all over the news. But our sources are picking up other chatter—political conflict, government instability, military dissatisfaction. It's a very unstable part of the world. I've been trying to persuade Victoria to return home. But she won't listen to reason."

"She always had a mind of her own. Besides, why *should* she come home? Obviously life is good."

The congressman slammed his hand down on the desk. "I'm telling you life is about to come tumbling down like a house of cards in Crimea. But the only one she'll listen to is Ian Keller. She practically worships him. He's smooth—almost hypnotic. Frankly, the man is lecherous—pure filth. But he covers his tracks. Victoria can't see it.

"As for Prince Peter—his ambition is frightening, unpredictable. But Victoria doesn't recognize that danger either. All she can see is the charm and power of royalty. I'm afraid of what a young woman in love might do."

Paladin considered for a moment and then turned the photograph over again to study the face of the girl. He smiled. "You know the trouble with you, Chase? You never had any confidence in Victoria. But I do. She's not stupid. I really don't think this is the kind of 'Prince Charming' she'd fall for. And even if she *did* have a crush on him, I wouldn't worry." He looked at the congressman. "She'll get over it by the senior prom."

Chase was suddenly livid, shouting, "Are you listening to me, Smith? I want Victoria out of Crimea!"

"So order her home!" Paladin shouted back. "Revoke her passport! Send the Marines!"

"I have no authority or legal justification to do any of those things."

"So go get her yourself."

"She has no respect for me," Chase managed to choke out.

"Well, neither do I," answered Paladin. He stood from his seat. As far as he was concerned, this ridiculous interview was over.

"But I think she respects you." Chase was quiet now, almost pleading. "I think she would come back if you asked her to."

Paladin paused, confused. "So—what? You want me to write her a letter?"

The congressman stood to face him. He swallowed. "I want you to go and bring her home."

Paladin froze and looked at him askew. "Are you out of your mind?"

Ignoring the remark, Chase leafed through the file on the desk, drawing out a document. "We—here it is—took the liberty of securing you a visa. I know you have a passport."

"I've also got a job."

"I've already made arrangements for a substitute, starting next week—as well as total security for your position until you return." The congressman paused from the full-court press and smiled nervously. "Remember, I have influence."

But Paladin had no intention of being railroaded. "I've got a wife now too. Don't you find it a little inappropriate, sending a married man to retrieve a single woman?"

"Not in the least," Chase answered without hesitation. "You're happily married—and you're a religious man. Two good reasons I can trust you."

"Your standards *have* changed," said Paladin.

23

Chase felt the rebuke but again resisted the impulse to react. He grew serious again. "I'll sweeten the pot, Smith." He pulled an envelope out of his coat pocket and extended it to Paladin. When Paladin recoiled slightly the congressman laid the envelope on the open manila folder. "I'll give you ten thousand dollars cash on the barrelhead for one week's work. You and your wife could use that on a teacher's salary, couldn't you?" Paladin looked silently at the envelope and then up at Chase.

The congressman continued. "There's also a one-way ticket to Rostov, Crimea, in that folder. The flight departs a week from tomorrow. Oh, and this." He retrieved a platinum bankcard from his inside coat pocket and dropped it on the growing pile atop the desk. "It's a debit card in your name to an account containing another ten thousand dollars for any expenses as well as return travel arrangements for the two of you."

Paladin shook his head slowly.

Chase spoke again, almost pleading. "Smith, if this opportunity could make up for the past—"

"It can't."

"But would you consider it, for Victoria's sake? She's in grave danger, and I'm running out of time." Keaton's hand appeared between them holding a business card. "Give Keaton here a call in the next twenty-four hours and let my office know."

Paladin took the card and ripped it in two. "And how do I contact you directly?"

Chase frowned and dug out a card of his own. "I'll give you some final instructions when you get ahold of me. Everything else you need is in the file." As Chase spoke, Keaton gathered the file together and placed it into a leather valise, handing it to Paladin.

Paladin ignored the valise. He took the business card and studied it. "I understand you're running for the senate next year." He looked up at Chase, void of emotion. "I intend to vote for the other guy." The congressman made no response.

At that instant a bell rang in the hallway. Paladin was unceremonious. "Gentlemen, you'll have to excuse me. I have some *important* people coming." He grabbed the valise and tossed it casually onto the lectern as the first student of his next hour came through the door. "Mr. Smith! I'm back!"

Mr. Smith turned to the boy. "Andrew! Good to see you!" He looked back to his visitors. "Gentlemen?"

From that moment, Mr. Smith ceased to acknowledge them. As the students entered he greeted them enthusiastically. The congressman and his assistant might as well have been furniture. Without ceremony they left the classroom and exited into the hallway.

—

The two men walked down the hallway in silence. A few late stragglers dashed past them as they pushed open the outside door and descended the stairs. Keaton finally spoke. "He's a hard character to figure out, sir. Not easy to deal with."

"I didn't expect him to be easy. But I think he'll take care of my problem."

"You're taking quite a chance—entrusting him with that kind of money."

"It'll be worth every penny. Besides, he may be difficult, but he's honest. No, the money is in perfectly safe hands."

"Yes, but will he go?"

"Oh, he'll go all right—for at least three reasons. In the first place, he needs that money. Second, if you heard anything about his life, you know he won't be able to resist the adventure."

"And what's the third reason?"

"The third reason is his nature. You see, Paladin Smith is just that—a paladin. A chivalrous knight, a heroic champion, a defender of a noble cause. In spite of his callous exterior, he'll never abandon a woman he perceives to be in distress—especially this one. No, Keaton, trust me. Our Mr. Smith fully intends to rescue Victoria Grant."

# 2

## Promise at Twilight

RACHEL SMITH SAT at the dining room table and stared silently at the envelope in front of her. Paladin stood across from her, leaning on the buffet against the wall. His mute attention was also focused on the stuffed envelope. The grandfather clock in the entry was the only sound accentuating the uncomfortable lack of conversation. All discussion regarding the object on the table had exhausted itself over twenty minutes ago.

The squeak of the back door hinges broke the silence, and a shaft of light from the setting sun flooded across the table. "Sorry that took so long." Paladin's father sauntered in from the patio followed by an excited mongrel terrier. "Come on, Sparky!" The old man carried a small dish of sizzling hamburgers in one hand and a plate of buns in the other. He paused at the table, looked between the two of them, and then at the envelope—the undisputable center of their attention. The only acknowledgment of his presence was the dog, who whimpered anxiously for a scrap of ground beef.

He cleared his throat. "Uh, would you mind if I, uh, moved that?" he asked politely.

Rachel looked up, awakened from her thoughts. "Hmm? Oh, no, Dad. Go ahead."

Harold Smith set down the plate of buns. He picked up the barbecue fork from the burger dish and jabbed the package aside like a piece of junk mail, then set the burgers on the center of the table in its place. "Weather's getting cold a little early this year. Won't be many good days for barbecuing left." He looked around at the empty place settings. "Paladin, you didn't set the table."

"Oh, right. Sorry, Dad. I've got a few things on my mind." He backed into the kitchen.

"Let me help," said Rachel. "I'll get the burger stuff."

"And something to drink," called out Harold, who was now alone with the dog in the dining room. He sat, closed his eyes, and briefly bowed his head.

"What'll it be, Dad? Paper or plastic?"

The old man's head popped up again. "Get the fine china, Son. It's not every day of the week I have you two over for dinner." As he spoke he reached over to the buffet for some napkins and placed one in front of each chair. His guests returned from the kitchen a moment later with the paper plates, utensils, and condiments. They sat expectantly. "Let's just dive in," announced Harold. "It's already been blessed."

Paladin smiled, then glanced at the overdone burgers. "Is that supposed to help?"

"You know what makes your wife a better dinner guest than you? She never complains about the food." Harold looked around again. "Did you bring out any glasses?"

Paladin sighed in frustration. "Dad, I'm a bit preoccupied tonight, okay?"

"A bit? You've both been sitting here staring at that package for the past half hour. The power of its contents has thrown the two of you into total analysis paralysis." The old man dangled a piece of hamburger over the dog, who took one snap and inhaled it in a single bite. "Good dog, Sparky."

"Well, it is a fair amount of cash, Dad," stepped in Rachel. "That's hard to ignore."

"I'll give you that," said Harold. "It's certainly more money than I've ever seen in one place." He paused thoughtfully. "Can I touch it?"

"Be my guest," offered Paladin.

"Why do you suppose he offered you so much?" Rachel asked, half to herself.

"Why do you suppose he offered it in cash?" added Harold, as he opened the flap gingerly and peered inside.

"That *has* bothered me," muttered Paladin. "The whole thing seemed a little 'cloak and dagger,' if you know what I mean."

"If you want my opinion," ventured the old man, easing back into his chair, "I don't think the good congressman wants any of this traceable back to him."

"Why?" asked Rachel.

Paladin shrugged. "That, I don't know."

"Paladin." Rachel looked steadily at him. "Can you trust Philip Chase?"

"Of course not," said Paladin. "He's a congressman. He lies for a living."

"Not totally," said Harold. "He told the truth about one thing. Crimea is a powder keg that's ready to explode. Little wonder he wants his niece out of there. The missionaries were forced to leave the country about a year ago. If what he says about this Keller or Prince What's-His-Name is true, I can understand his concern. What I can't understand is—" He cut himself off abruptly.

Suddenly the room was quiet. "What, Dad?" asked Rachel.

"Why I feel so uncomfortable about it."

"Frankly, I don't feel so good about it myself," Paladin said flatly, looking at the congressman's card.

"Well, that's a good place to start," said his father. "But what exactly don't you feel good about?"

"Does it matter?" Paladin reasoned, "Dad, you've always taught me that feelings are the language of the Spirit. So why shouldn't I follow mine? Why shouldn't I follow yours?"

"Well, as far as your feelings are concerned, you need to make sure which part is bothering you—the congressman or the quest? It's easy to get the two confused. As far as my feelings are concerned, you can't get my inspiration mixed up with your own in this matter. It isn't my place to make this decision for you or to even influence you. I haven't been asked to make this journey, that money hasn't been offered to me, and your life isn't mine."

There was a long silence at the table as Paladin looked at his father. The old man just smiled. Rachel finally spoke. "What about the girl, Paladin?"

"What *about* her?"

"She needs to get out of Crimea. If you go, will she listen to you? Can you make a difference?"

"It's possible," he answered, more to himself than anyone else.

Rachel looked at the old man for a response. Her pleading expression begged for him to break the tense silence. He raised his eyes slowly to look at his son and finally spoke. "Then maybe everything else *is* irrelevant—the congressman, the money, the mad journey across half the globe. Maybe the girl is all that matters."

Paladin looked at him with a dull, searching expression.

"Like I said," his father added, "my opinion is really inconsequential here. I'm just an old man. Maybe you two should find out what the Lord thinks. That is an opinion that *does* make all the difference." Standing from the table, Harold picked up a burned, cold burger from the plate and took a huge bite. "Well, I hate to eat and run," he announced with his mouth full, "but this is a perfect time for my evening constitutional. I'm going for a walk. I'll leave the rest of the burgers and the house to you."

He bowed slightly and stepped to the front door. "Come on, Sparky." A moment later man and dog were both gone with the door shut behind them. Paladin and Rachel were alone.

There was another long silence in the room as Rachel looked at him. "I know you, Paladin. You're going, aren't you?"

"It'll only be a week. I'll go, find her, bring her home—I hope—and be back with you in no time."

Again the only sound in the house was the clock in the entryway. "What was she like, Paladin? Victoria . . ."

"Grant," Paladin finished the name for her. "Just a girl. A student. Seventeen years old. Outgoing and very social, but a little insecure under the circumstances. Intelligent though, and talented."

"What did she look like?"

Paladin took a picture from his shirt pocket and handed it across the table to her. She raised her eyebrows and took it. It was a snapshot of a row of students, posed and seated at their desks. On the back of the snapshot were brief notes about each student. Brother Smith had taken a picture of each row in every one of his classes since he began teaching, years ago.

Rachel studied the photograph. Sitting in the second seat back was a wholesome-looking girl with shoulder-length auburn hair, smiling at the camera. She wore a blanket and a pair of pajamas. Her features showed fatigue, but she was still radiant. Rachel glanced up at her husband and smiled.

"Remember," he answered, "this was early morning seminary. She's probably a little haggard."

"Nonsense," commented Rachel, "she's very pretty. A natural. She has beautiful eyes."

Paladin reached over and lifted the snapshot from her hand with two fingers. "Chase gave me a more recent photo if you'd like to see it."

"No," said Rachel, "I don't need to. *This* girl would only get prettier. I just wanted to see her as *you* remembered her."

"Frankly, I *couldn't* remember—exactly. That's why I had to go digging through my archives."

"Did she have a crush on you, Paladin?"

"I guess so. I suppose it's worn off by now."

"Worn off?" She chuckled. "Oh, Darling, you have no idea what you're up against."

"I beg your pardon?"

"Paladin,"—Rachel propped her chin on her folded fingers—"your father talks about danger. But you may be in more peril than you'll ever know. If I know women, she's not only *over* you, she probably despises you. You turned on your innocent charisma, rode your white charger to the rescue, captured her heart at the height of her mature adolescence, and then abandoned her—vanishing without so much as a farewell to punctuate the tragedy of it all. There can be no greater betrayal than the one you've committed to shatter a romantic fantasy. A girl can't even put that in her diary. And from there—'Hell hath no fury like a teenage woman's scorn.'"

Paladin held up the snapshot. "*This* is a teenage woman's scorn?"

Rachel smiled, a twinkle in her eye. "It's got potential."

Paladin considered, looking from Rachel to the snapshot and back again. "Then why are you letting me fly into this hurricane?"

The smile half disappeared from Rachel's face. "Because she *still* needs you. And because if she's anything like me, she'll take one look at that charming, disarming face of yours and forgive everything for old times sake. Your mission will be accomplished. And you'll be home again."

Paladin slipped the photo back into his pocket and leaned toward Rachel. "Then you're not jealous?"

"Sweetheart, if I got jealous of every pretty face in your classes—where every year every girl is always going to be seventeen—I'd be a basket case. Besides, none of them can have the crush on you—or the faith in you—that I do." She stopped and collected herself. "I'll miss you."

"For a week?" He tried to lighten the atmosphere. "I've gone off with the Boy Scouts at summer camp for that long."

"Paladin, be serious," she halfheartedly scolded. "Do you realize where Crimea is?"

"I *did* look it up on the map."

"So did I. It's over six thousand miles away on the other side of the world. And your dad *is* right. It's the dangerous side of the world."

"Rachel, if you don't want me to go . . ."

"It's not that." She was in serious earnest now. "It will never come to that. When I married you I knew you were something special. Someone with a gift and a destiny, with a calling to serve the Lord—and a place to fill in the world. I know some of those places we're going to see together. But others you're going to have to fill alone."

"Rachel, I don't think—"

"Let me finish. I vowed when you asked me to marry you that I was not going to be a clingy wife who was going to get in the way of what you had to do. Well, I haven't had to sacrifice much yet. Scoutmaster, priesthood advisor, seminary teacher—they haven't asked that much of you so far. But the day is coming when more responsibilities and greater leadership is going to be placed upon you. I can't tell the future, but I know the time is coming when I'm going to have to give you up to something higher." She looked squarely at him. "I don't know, darling. This seems like that kind of a call."

"From Congressman Philip Chase?"

Her smile was enigmatic. "God moves in mysterious ways. And he loves surprises. At any rate, I'm not going to start holding you back and being selfish now—especially if there is someone out there who truly needs you. And I feel there is. But remember,

Paladin Smith, you come home, because no one in this world needs you more than I do."

Paladin suddenly stood from his chair at the table and stepped over to Rachel. Lifting her from her seat, he wrapped her in his arms and kissed her. She embraced him warmly. Neither spoke for a long minute as they held each other.

Finally he pulled away just far enough to look into her eyes. "I'll come home," he spoke in a whisper. "I promise."

"I'll be waiting."

As he stared at her in the twilight, a smile stole across his lips, and he put his finger in the air as if to suggest he had an idea.

"What?" she said.

Moving quickly to his father's old stereo unit he looked through the albums on the shelf and pulled one out. "You know my dad is old fashioned, but right now I'm feeling a little sentimental myself." He carefully removed a large vinyl disk from its jacket and placed it on the turntable. Then he cautiously placed the needle on the record.

There were a few slight pops from the scratches, but when the music began, the richness of a full orchestra filled the room with a romantic melody as Paladin rushed to Rachel and took her in a formal dancing pose. "Madam," he said, holding her close, "shall we dance?"

Rachel chuckled playfully as Paladin began to awkwardly sway and move her slowly around the table. He nodded, and, as if by invitation, the effortless voice of Nat King Cole joined the orchestra in a perfect blend of music and lyrics.

> *When I fall in love, it will be forever*
> *Or I'll never fall in love . . .*

The pure refinement of every note stood out in sheer contrast to Paladin's lack of grace. Rachel's smile grew broader. "We really need to teach you to dance," she said. Paladin joined her, laughing at himself, but only momentarily. They both sobered as they gazed at each other. The rich and mellow music continued to etch the words of the song in the air and into their memories.

*And the moment that I feel that you feel that way too*
*Is when I fall in love with you.*

# 3

## INTO THE UNKNOWN

**P** **ALADIN SAT BACK** in his seat on the Aeroflot 767 and contemplated the flight ahead of him as the plane lifted from the runway at Los Angeles International Airport. He occupied a spot in the center section of the economy cabin between the two aisles. The size of the plane made no impact on passenger comfort, only on capacity—and it was going to be an uncomfortable, cramped fifteen-hour journey.

Culture shock was also going to settle in on his way across the world. Russian was the idiom of choice among his fellow passengers, and there was very little second-language accommodation for unschooled Westerners.

Paladin craned his neck to scan his surroundings now that the flight was underway. The most fascinating feature of economy class was a large, elevated projection screen about twenty feet away at the front of the cabin. On it were cast regular images—maps of the journey and GPS locations of the plane as it raced across two oceans and two continents. That picture was an anchor to Paladin as he considered the eerie and incredible concept that he was traversing some six thousand miles of the globe in less time than it would take him to drive from LA to Denver. A day's travel would find him in a world vastly different from the one he knew.

Life had a way of changing drastically when you went too far from home. Events in the mission field in Argentina had changed his life forever. His years on the road discovering America had changed his life again. Now suddenly he was being thrust into another world where the potential for change was huge, mysterious, and seemingly inescapable. The thought frightened him. He shook his head as if to clear away the static. What was he thinking? This was just a short trip. He'd be back in a few days and that would be the end of it.

Still Paladin couldn't erase his father's words from his memory. Not that he wanted to. He had asked his father for a blessing,[3] as he had at so many crossroads of his life, because he was in need of comfort, and strength, and a certain confidence amid confusion. And he respected his dad. He considered him a man of God whose advice and spiritual direction had always been a guiding star. His father had consented gratefully.

It was Sunday night. He and Rachel both arrived at the old man's house and retired to the den where there was a reverent quiet insulated by walls of books. Blessings in this room by the family patriarch were traditional. But Harold Smith was different that night. He was more subdued than normal. He'd been fasting and praying. He said he felt he needed to especially prepare this time. He began.

"Paladin Smith, by the authority of the Holy Melchizedek Priesthood, I place my hands upon your head to give you a father's blessing."

The old man spoke of his love for him, the blessings God had

---

3. Latter-day Saint fathers who have been ordained to the Melchizedek Priesthood may pronounce special blessings on their families.

given him, and the satisfaction of heaven with his dedication to the gospel and to the work of the Lord. But then his father paused. When he resumed, the blessing took on a tone that surprised both Paladin and Rachel—as well as the old man.

"Paladin, it is no accident that you have been called to go to this foreign land at this time. The assignment that has been placed upon your shoulders is the will of God. The mission you embark upon cannot be foreseen with your present sight and intellect. But know that in accomplishing that which is before you, you will alter the lives of thousands and millions."

In that instant, Paladin had practically burst from his seat. He heard Rachel gasp, and his father paused again. What was he saying! He wasn't called, and this wasn't a mission! He was merely going to help an old friend. That was all.

His father resumed, warning him of dangerous lands and the evil designs of men in high places. Of journeys and perils and quests.

"But be not dismayed. This is your Father's work and He will bestow you with gifts of the Spirit to meet the challenges that you face. However, you must be diligent to be worthy of them, seek them with all your heart, and utilize them with all your strength."

A jolt of turbulence brought Paladin back to the present. He blinked his eyes and looked across the aisle through one of the cabin windows. Having taken off into the evening twilight, the plane was still climbing north as the sky quickly darkened. It seemed appropriate to be soaring into the dead of night. Such was the unknown of his adventure—that had become some kind of a mission. He tried to remember more of his father's words of counsel.

"Beware the temptation to rely on the wisdom of man or the arm of flesh. Your only true foundation is the Lord, and your confidence shall wax strong in his presence."

Words of scripture echoed in Paladin's mind. *Trust in the Lord with all thine heart,* he thought, *and lean not unto thine own understanding. In all thy ways acknowledge him, and he shall direct thy paths.*

Finally, his father concluded.

"Paladin, do not let pride, carelessness, or the desires of the flesh rob you of the blessings that the Lord seeks to shower upon your head. Satan will feel after you to destroy you. But the Lord Jesus Christ will be your defense and refuge.

"May you let his Spirit guide you in all things until you return.

"I seal these blessings upon you in the name of Jesus Christ, amen."

When the blessing was over and the old man removed his hands, Paladin sat motionless and heaved a deep sigh before he opened his eyes. "Dad," he said, "I've never received a blessing like that."

Paladin's father took out a handkerchief, wiped a bead of perspiration from his brow, and fell into a nearby cushioned chair. "In my whole life, son, I've never *given* a blessing like that."

Then Paladin looked at Rachel. She was crying.

The soft beep of the cabin alarm startled Paladin to reality again. It was a signal to the passengers that they could unfasten their restraints and roam at will. Rachel. He missed her already. They hadn't talked a lot in the airport before his flight. There was a great deal on both their minds—an emotional mixture of anticipation and anxiety. But most of it had already been said.

"There shouldn't be anything to worry about," he reassured her.

She smiled. "Then why do you keep saying that?"

"I'm just going over everything in my mind," he said, running his fingers through his hair. "I hope I haven't forgotten anything. I mean, here at home, for you."

"You haven't." She squeezed his hand. "We've got money in the bank, I've got your dad around in case there's an emergency, and overall I can fend for myself." She paused. "Just call me or drop me an email every day."

He laughed, and they embraced and kissed.

He smiled to himself on the plane. Then he grew serious. *Money in the bank.* He supposed five thousand dollars and their savings would be enough for any eventuality—for a week at any rate. If it was to be just a week. Why he brought any of that cash with him on this short journey he didn't quite know. Even now the pouch that hung around his neck under his sweater weighed heavily. Safely tucked within it were fifty crisp, clean, unfolded one-hundred dollar bills and the debit card that he'd received from Congressman Chase.

His mind reflected on the conversation he'd had with his father, who felt so strongly about him taking the money. "Five thousand dollars is a lot of cash to carry with me, Dad. Why shouldn't I just leave all this for Rachel? After all Chase gave me the debit card for spending money."

"I thought you didn't trust the congressman?"

"All right. But even at that, I just don't feel comfortable carrying five thousand dollars in currency. Wouldn't I be smarter to convert it into travelers' checks?"

"Maybe. Maybe not," said the old man. "Remember, you're going to Crimea. You never know what they'll think of American Express, but good economy or bad, they'll always love the American dollar." Then he stopped. "Besides all that, I just feel you ought to take the money. I wish you could take more. But that will have to do."

Paladin sat in the plane and heaved another deep, thoughtful sigh. His father had been so serious about the issue that he hadn't argued, especially after Sunday's blessing. His hand went to his chest where he felt the pouch under his sweater. In some things he had simply learned to trust his father.

He glanced up at the GPS map. The plane was heading northeast through the Rocky Mountain States on a course that would take them through Canada. Air speed—550 mph. Outside temperature—forty degrees below zero. Shaking his head, he adjusted the scarf around his neck, opened his book on American history, and began to read. Others around him were conversing quietly in Russian or browsing through newspapers.

Gradually, heads began to nod and overhead lights went out. Soon Paladin seemed to be the only person awake in the cabin. The sky was pitch black through the window across the aisle. Paladin squinted up at the GPS screen. The plane had flown through the corner of Saskatchewan and was well into Manitoba heading toward a place called Churchill on the shores of the Hudson Bay. Air speed—610 mph. Outside temperature seventy-nine degrees below zero. Wow. Paladin shivered, closed his book, and decided to take a nap. Unfolding an airlines blanket, he pulled it up around his chest, cinched the scarf tight under his chin, and dozed off.

It was a good rest but only a few hours long. When he eased awake, he looked around. Most people were still asleep. The light from the windows caught his attention. Daylight. He took a quick look at his watch: 2:15 a.m. Of course, it was daylight. The airplane was flying east, racing headlong into tomorrow—meeting the morning. The time on his watch no longer meant anything, not up here. He looked at the GPS map to get his bearings. The 767 was now soaring high over Baffin Bay in North Canada, well above the 60th parallel. Out there was the land of the midnight sun. Paladin was in another world now.

He pulled the blanket away, unfastened his safety belt, and stood stiffly. He crouched to peer out the windows. He couldn't see a thing here, directly over the wings.

He made his way toward the rear of the plane where no one was seated for the moment, leaned over, and squinted into the morning light. Twenty thousand feet below lay an eerie fantasy—a sheet of ice as far as the eye could see, crazed and cracked like an old plate of china. His gaze followed the broken pattern in the distance until it disappeared into the fog. He smiled in fascination as he returned to his place, continuing to take an additional glance through every unshuttered window.

Paladin eased into his seat, careful not to wake those he was sitting next to. He sat for several minutes staring at the screen, contemplating the stark diversity of the world he lived in. The plane was approaching the coast of Greenland. Airspeed—590 mph. Outside temperature—sixty-one degrees below zero. It was warming up.

The cabin was still quiet. Paladin stretched and reached into his briefcase that was stowed under the seat in front of him. Fumbling inside he retrieved the valise he'd received from Chase a week ago. He'd already been through the packet of materials a couple of times. But considering that the information they held could make the difference between life and death, one more time couldn't hurt. He unsnapped the valise and opened it to reveal the familiar manila file. Unfolding it he began to page through its contents.

The first photograph was that of Ian Keller and Victoria Grant. He preferred to ignore Keller for the present. But he paused for a long moment to consider his pretty former student. What *would* she be like? He'd thrown the picture of seventeen-year-old Victoria into the file with the young adult version. He picked it up and compared the two. She really hadn't changed, only grown more mature. Paladin wondered what scars the world had inflicted since high school. *But then again, we all have those. They're called time—and life.* He'd find out soon enough.

His eyes drifted to Keller. He winced. He turned to the next photograph of the suave, oily ambassador. What was it that Paladin instinctively disliked about him? He knew it wasn't right to judge a man on pure appearance. But then again, there was something about Keller that simply wasn't right. It was inescapable. And Keller was the key to Crimea. He put down the photograph and leafed through the State Department summaries. "Here it is." He reviewed the data in his mind.

*Crimea*
*Area—120,050 square miles. Population—43,542,000.*

41

*Basic history—Crimea separated themselves from the Soviet Union along with Ukraine and Georgia the summer of 1991. Assembled members of the Crimean Parliament officially declared themselves an independent state ten days later. First democratic elections held in December of that year. Independence ratified by over 90 percent of the people.*

*Government—Constitutional monarchy. Parliamentary structure. Executive authority—prime minister. Current elected leader—Yuri Tiomkin, former Chairman of Labor Party in Parliament. Elected two years ago for a five-year term.*

Paladin turned the page to see a Xerox photo of an aging gentleman in a sash addressing a legislative body. He looked at the picture for a moment and shrugged. The man seemed to be the image of distinguished service in any country. He turned back the page to continue.

*Titular head—Pyotr (Peter) Vasiliyevich, prince of Crimea, ("Peter the Great"). Vasiliyevich has no legitimate political power but significant influence with the people as a traditional and ceremonial head of state.*

"Something like the royalty of England," Paladin reasoned. He dug out the photo of Victoria and Peter to study the face of the prince. What he saw, however, was something he never saw on the faces of the royalty of England. Pure arrogance and ostentation—all dressed up and nowhere to go. As he'd noticed before, this man really thought he was in charge of something, or was determined to be. Paladin continued.

*Military—With the dissolution of the Soviet Union, Crimea found itself in control of a huge military, including over 600,000 soldiers, significant ongoing defense capabilities, and the fifth largest nuclear arsenal in the world.*

Paladin's eyes popped out of his head. How could he have missed that before? He read on.

*Undisputed head of the military is Colonel Dimitri Ustinov, whose loyalties are closely aligned with the royal family.*

Paladin quickly flipped through the next pages to find the photo of a stern-faced, middle-aged man in uniform who you wouldn't want to ask traffic directions from. Paladin shivered.

*Religion—Overwhelmingly Russian Orthodox. Head of the church in Crimea for the past fifteen years is Archbishop Basil II. In spite of widespread esteem of the Crimean people, he limits his sphere of influence to religious matters. Is politically moderate and traditionally loyal to the royal house.*

Paladin was fascinated by this man. He flipped through the pages to glance at the face of an elderly man with a long white beard, dressed in a black robe and cap, with a chain of authority hanging around his neck. He actually looked quite saintly. Still, wasn't he among those that had demanded the Mormon missionaries leave the country? Hmm.

Now for the ugly part.

*Economy—Like the Soviet Union itself and the rest of her satellites, Crimea had imploded on the economic house of cards, which had been the foundation of unsound Communist principles. "Economic slowdown was followed by inflation and hyperinflation, all taking their toll, breaking down the stability of the nation," read the report.*

"The wonder of Communism." Paladin shook his head. "You can't violate the economic laws of nature and escape the consequences." The problem with a bad economy was the effect it had on everything else—and the kind of people it lured in, anxious to seize control. "Like vultures circling around a dying carcass," he whispered aloud, "ready for the feast."

He thought of the giant Russian Federation looming just north of Crimea, more than anxious to engulf nations like Ukraine, Georgia, and Crimea back into a new and reborn monster state. Alexander Trotsky, the president of Russia, had been flexing his muscles in experimental ways for a few years now.

Paladin reached back in a pocket of the valise and pulled out an Internet article on President Trotsky. It wasn't part of the State Department materials. The subject wasn't one they liked to openly talk about. Trotsky was a "friend." But his designs and ambitions on his southern neighbors were fairly transparent. Crimea and the other mineral and agriculturally rich states of Eastern Europe had abandoned the Russian family. Now Trotsky desperately wanted the prodigals to return—peaceably, or otherwise. And the time was now ripe to do so.

Crimea had been leaning toward a relationship with the North Atlantic Treaty Organization, and, along with NATO, a permanent alliance with the West. But an uncertain economy, civil turmoil, military threats, and a political tug-of-war between the parliament and the prince had postponed the national referendum on NATO. How much Russia was responsible for Crimea's present instability was unclear. "Vulture," muttered Paladin to himself as he stared at Trotsky's steel-faced photo in the article.

Paladin thought of all the faces he'd been studying—Alexander Trotsky, Prince Pyotr, Colonel Ustinov—potential vultures every one. And of course there was Keller. Ian Keller who, according to the State Department, was the glue "influential enough to hold opposing parties apart and American interests together in Crimea."

He remembered Congressman Chase's words. *We need people like Keller. He's useful.* Paladin took another look at the photograph of Ambassador Keller. He could easily imagine him as a dealer in Vegas or a salesman in a used car lot. What exactly was Keller holding together and what exactly did he want with Victoria Grant?

*Vulture,* he thought again as he closed the file and shut the leather valise. He carefully replaced the entire package back inside his briefcase under the seat in front of him and took another long stretch. Only now did he realize that most of the passengers in the cabin were awake. The morning of their body clocks had dawned. Light streamed through the windows and many were milling about to get their blood circulating again.

At the far end of the cabin, flight attendants were rolling their way toward him with dinner, which was actually breakfast. It seemed appropriate that the food itself was as unidentifiable as the mealtime they were observing.

Paladin dutifully partook of the international mystery meat and the warmed over vegetables—universal airline fare—to stave off the hunger. But nothing hit the spot in a satisfying way. He couldn't wait to get the tray off his cramped lap space.

He leaned back his seat and closed his eyes for a few minutes but took no more than a short power nap before he was alert again. He simply couldn't relax. He stood and took a stroll to the nearest empty window seat. The jumbo jet was now flying over the breadth of Greenland, a vast landscape of ice and snow, broken only by occasional mountains and irregular ruts that may have been courses of travel.

Satisfied, he returned to his place, but part of him was still restless. Paladin needed to ease and unburden his mind a little. Frankly, he'd been busy, but he couldn't afford to let himself get this distracted—and he knew what he'd been neglecting. He opened the overhead compartment and took out the carrying case that held his scriptures before nestling back into his seat. Unzipping the case, he removed and opened the Book of Mormon. But out of the inside cover fell an envelope he'd placed there for safekeeping.

He smiled. Another momentary distraction—as well it should have been. No document in his possession, including his passport or visa, had been harder to come by or seemed more valuable.

"What do you mean a letter of introduction?" Chase had asked him.

"Nothing in that packet gives me any justification for being six thousand miles from home in hostile territory," argued Paladin, "except for ten thousand dollars and the shadow of your smile."

"Isn't that enough?" protested the congressman. "What do you need a letter for?"

"Because if everything doesn't go smoothly, which is highly likely, I want something to fall back on." He paused. "Congressman, surely a little three-line letter can't be that big of a problem." Paladin had the distinct impression that, in Chase's entire legal and political career, he had never made any concession less willingly.

The letter, delivered by Keaton the next day, was terse and official, typed on House of Representatives stationery. It read:

> *To whom it may concern,*
>
>     *This letter is to present Mr. Paladin Smith to United States Ambassador Ian Keller at the American Embassy in Rostov, Crimea. Mr. Smith will explain his business with you upon his arrival.*
>
>     *(signed)*
>
>     *Philip Chase*
>
>     *House of Representatives*
>
>     *United States of America*

Paladin smiled again and carefully replaced the letter in the envelope and returned it to the inside cover of his triple combination.

He took one more glance up at the GPS screen to see that the plane had left the empty expanse of Greenland and was now flying over the equally empty expanse of the Norwegian Sea. They had been in the air for almost ten hours now.

Paladin opened to 1 Nephi[4] and began to read. He read and forgot about the flight, the map on the wall, the thousands of feet of space below him, and the strange mission ahead. His mind and spirit drifted to another time, to the journey of a family, to the quest of a young man, and to the whispered commands of God that changed the world.

He read intently, lost in the adventure, the words, and the simple faith in Jesus Christ that moved and still moves in the lives of ordinary men and women—allowing them to do the impossible. Pages turned and chapter after chapter passed before his eyes until gradually, almost imperceptibly, his eyes gently closed, and he fell into a peaceful sleep.

When Paladin slowly opened his eyes a few hours later, the 767 had passed through the latitudes over Scandinavia and well into the air space of Eastern Russia, heading south. He became instantly awake and looked at the map on the cabin wall. Mockba— Moscow was north and west of them. How long had he slept? He strained a look at his watch. 8:15 a.m., LA time. Who knew what time it was on the ground? Air speed—475 mph. Outside temperature—forty-five degrees below. Altitude—15,000 feet. The airplane was gradually descending, making a slow approach to his ultimate destination: Rostov, the capital city of Crimea, a few hundred miles ahead.

The minutes crept by as Paladin again contemplated the experience that awaited him. Soon the GPS jet was almost on top of the city point on the map. The passengers were asked to return to their seats. Paladin's ears were stopped up. He held his nose and popped them. Yes, the plane was descending rapidly now. Rostov

---

4. "1 Nephi" is the first book in the Book of Mormon. Accepted as ancient scripture by The Church of Jesus Christ of Latter-day Saints, the Book of Mormon tells of God's dealings with the ancient inhabitants of the American continent and the visit of Jesus Christ to them after his resurrection. Nephi is the major heroic character in the opening chapters of the book who is commanded by God to flee Jerusalem with his family prior to the Babylonian captivity.

was below them. He could see it through the window up ahead and across the aisle. The Book of Mormon still lay open on his lap. He took the covers to close it, but the book slipped from his hands and fell open again to 1 Nephi 4. Paladin found himself staring at verse six—a scripture he'd underlined long ago. The three lines suddenly spoke volumes to him:

> *And I was led by the Spirit, not knowing beforehand the things which I should do.*

Quietly, Paladin shut the book and held it on his lap with his eyes closed. Minutes went by as he uttered a silent prayer. Then he felt the jolt of the landing gear grabbing the runway as the plane touched down and rolled to a long stop.

Still, he clenched his eyes tight. *Dear Lord*, he thought in a heartfelt plea, *whatever am I doing here?*

# 4

## THE STILL SMALL VOICE

**P**ALADIN EXITED THE plane into the Rostov Terminal—a world which was not the least inclined to accommodate him. He passed through Crimean customs, showed his passport to the unsmiling uniformed officers behind several glass panels, and finally, with his luggage, rolled into what seemed to be an ocean of taxi drivers anxious to deliver him anywhere he wanted to go.

The trouble was, he had no idea where to go. He had to do some serious thinking to even figure out what day and time it was. What seemed morning to him was indeed late afternoon in Rostov. He'd lost half a day flying east. Tuesday was history and Wednesday was almost a thing of the past. The Crimean sun was already sinking into evening.

All of this only meant one question to Paladin Smith. How could he possibly find Victoria Grant at this time of day? The American Embassy was closed. There seemed nothing else for it but to check into a hotel for the night and begin his quest at square one in the morning. He needed to unwind anyway.

Paladin flagged one of the taxi drivers and asked him to take him to a good hotel. The driver understood that much English and agreed. The drive from the airport to the heart of the capital was a representative tour of a bleak Eastern European metropolis.

The taxi jostled for position among a million other automobiles, packed onto streets never designed for congested traffic. But the driver knew the twists and turns of every alley and driveway like a lab rat in a maze. Within twenty minutes he delivered Paladin to the front door of the Hotel Crimea—a classic, old style hotel that was guaranteed to provide every luxury at a hefty bill.

Paladin's experience in South America had taught him the art of haggling that could be adapted to any language. But he was fair with his driver and found, as his father had promised, that the American dollar was more than welcome, especially in hard cash.

He carried his own bags to the front desk where the clerk addressed him in clear English with just a hint of an accent. Paladin smiled, presented his passport, and the congressman's debit card—and found both honored as he was handed his key.

"How long will the gentleman be staying?" asked the clerk.

"I'm not quite sure," he answered. He wished he knew.

As a final word the clerk handed him a list of hotel perks. "You may wish to take advantage of the hotel's amenities during your stay," he said pleasantly. "There is five-star dining in our restaurant or more casual meals in our café. We also have a spa on the patio level. And, of course, there is dancing in the Caucasus Room until midnight."

Paladin smiled. "Thank you. I'm not very hungry. And as for dancing—well, you'd have to ask my wife. I'm a pretty hopeless case. Tonight I just want a good night's sleep."

"That we can guarantee you," the clerk said with a slight bow. "Good night, sir."

Paladin nodded wearily and picked up his luggage—an overnight bag and his briefcase. He was glad at this moment to be traveling light. As he struggled to the elevator, he heard the music blaring from the Caucasus Room not far away. Yes, there was quite a party going on in there. Not for him. It would be good to take a shower and crash for the night. He would start fresh in the morning.

The elevator door opened and Paladin stumbled inside. Only when the doors had closed and he was on his way to the fifth floor did the annoying music muffle and finally grow silent. He found suite 512 just around the corner from the elevator—a small, comfortable room with a view of the dull city lights, a hard bed, and a combination shower-tub with claw feet. It was plenty for him. All he asked was warm water to bathe in and a place to sleep.

In a half hour he was showered, and even shaved, and ready to call it a night. But as he lay in bed, he was suddenly wide awake. The sensation was very disappointing. In one sense he was exhausted. But in another, he couldn't turn off his brain thinking about tomorrow. How exactly *was* he going to find Victoria Grant? What was he going to say to her when he found her? And how in the world could he expect her to leave Crimea and return with him to America on this fool's errand?

Paladin threw back the covers and got out of bed. Lying there in a state of insomnia was such a waste of time. He turned on the desk light to read a little history. But even that activity failed to engage his mind. He slammed the book closed in frustration and walked to the closet where he'd hung his few clothes.

In less than five minutes he was outside the elevator door again, fully dressed—white shirt, tie, jacket, and scarf. It was early evening—eight or so, Rostov time. The night was still fresh. Paladin just wanted to get out. "What the heck is wrong with me?" He rubbed his eyes with his fingers. The elevator doors opened. The lift was going down. That was fine with him. It didn't matter. He pushed the ground floor button, and the doors closed again.

When the elevator doors opened again onto the lobby, Paladin remembered why he had been glad to leave a short time before. The dance music from the Caucasus Room continued to blare as if it were grad night. Maybe it was.

Paladin made a beeline to the exit doors of the hotel when he suddenly stopped at the entrance to the ballroom. He stood curiously and peered through the huge doors, strangely fascinated by the flashing lights, the pulsating beat, and the rock, break, and swing dancing inside.

This wasn't what he wanted to do tonight. The world through that doorway held no real interest for him. There was not a spirit in there that he really enjoyed. And yet he felt drawn into the ballroom, and not by any impulse that made him uncomfortable. It was hard for him to understand or explain. Something in his heart was compelling him through that entry. *Go on inside. It's all right.*

As he walked into the huge, darkened room, Paladin found himself enveloped in an atmosphere that made him instantly feel out of place. He was about to turn around when a sensation overwhelmed him. It was amazing. Suddenly and unmistakably—here, alone, and without his wife, surrounded by alcohol, immodesty, and irreverence—he felt totally girded in the armor of God.

He walked around the edge of the room, still not sure what had brought him here, but fascinated by the sights and sounds of Babylon all around him. He stopped to simply watch the lights.

"Anything to drink, sir?" droned the bartender in a thick Russian accent.

Paladin realized he was leaning on the bar. "Oh, no. No, thank you." He retreated awkwardly away a few steps. A few of the passing patrons glanced at him and smiled. His appearance as well as his demeanor made him slightly conspicuous in this crowd. He began to grow uncomfortable again. The armor of God tends to stand out on a dance floor.

"What am I doing here, Father?" he asked in a whisper. And again a wave of peace swept over him that seemed to say, *Be patient. All will be well.*

It struck Paladin as incongruent for the Spirit to be in such a place. He felt comforted. But then again, none of it made much sense. This was specifically the kind of place he'd been telling his students for years *not* to hang around in. Maybe it was time to go.

He began walking, in as straight a course as he could, back to the entryway. That took him partially onto the floor, but he was anxious at this point to simply leave. Not many people were dancing there anyway. One couple was salsa dancing, and pretty wildly too. But they could be avoided. So he thought.

Paladin glanced at them as they danced. The girl was graceful. Attired in a flowing, knee-length dress, she flawlessly followed every lead of her elegant partner. Together, the couple had captivated the attention of everyone in the room. The music was about over when they unexpectedly came gyrating in Paladin's direction, and with them, the admiring view of the watching crowd.

Spinning on her partner's right hand, the girl continued to move closer and closer to Paladin as he backed away, trying not to attract a scene. He needn't have worried. All eyes were on the lithe dancer, who was turning faster and faster in the young man's arms as the music sped to a climax.

Paladin was finally to the edge of the huge circle that the crowd had made for the couple. There was no place left to go, when all at once the music ended and the beauty fell into her partner's arms, with her slender body outstretched and the back of her head nearly touching the floor.

The entire room erupted into applause as she lay there panting, beaming, gazing up, first at the ceiling and then into the face of Paladin Smith. Paladin's mouth fell open in amazement. It was her! Victoria Grant! Paladin could not have been more shocked had the angel Moroni[5] collapsed in front of him.

But Victoria's reaction was beyond words. Her eyes grew instantly

---

5. The angel Moroni was the heavenly messenger who appeared to the Prophet Joseph Smith in 1823 to reveal the buried gold plates of the Book of Mormon.

the size of saucers as she strained her neck to look at Paladin right side up. And suddenly she wasn't the least bit graceful. She struggled to her feet, nervously acknowledged the applause, thanked her partner with a hug, and then turned to Paladin as the crowd began to filter away. She was still exhausted and breathing heavily.

"Brother Smith!" she panted, smoothing her dress and looking around as if the crowd was still watching. She squinted at him as if she might have made a mistake.

"Brother Smith?" This time she laughed nervously for a moment and then settled down to a more serious mood. "Brother Smith—Paladin Smith. It's you. I can't believe it. You look exactly the same. Exactly."

"Well, I should"—he laughed uncomfortably—"because it is me. And you—you look older. A good older. I mean you look perfect." He really couldn't think of a thing to say. After all the effort the Holy Ghost had spent to get him in here, his job was done. It was obviously true that the "Spirit will not always strive with man." Paladin was now definitely on his own.

"Do you remember me?" she asked. "I mean, do you know who I am?"

Paladin was flabbergasted. "Do I? Of course, I know . . . Victoria Grant. Victoria, you're the one I . . ." *Get a hold of yourself, Paladin,* he thought. *Don't overplay your hand.*

"What did you say?" she shouted. Paladin was grateful for the music now. It had begun without warning, interrupting all conversation, or what little conversation he was capable of.

"Listen, can we go into the lobby?" he yelled in response. Victoria smiled and nodded, her eyes sparkling. It was the look Paladin had now engraved in his memory of the girl, second seat from the front, in his early morning seminary class seven years ago. He gestured toward the entrance, and they walked together through the doorway and into the lobby. The music of the ballroom was barely behind them before she turned to him.

"So, what have you been doing? What are you doing in Crimea? I've got a million questions. And I've got so much to tell you." She fell into a lobby sofa and pulled Paladin down enthusiastically beside her. "Sit down and tell me everything."

If this were a young woman scorned, Paladin didn't recognize it. Obviously Rachel was wrong. She was in a good enough mood. Now, if he could just kidnap her and get her on a plane back to America tonight, this whole affair would be over.

"Oh, you've heard all my stories before," he demurred. "Let's talk about you. Are you married?"

She laughed aloud. "Are you kidding? No way! I've got a career, Brother Smith. A real career."

So she wasn't interested in getting married to anybody, even a prince. That was good news.

"You know how I always wanted to go into government? Well, I made it. I'm here in Crimea working for the US Embassy. It's great!"

"Wow!" he said encouragingly. "What kind of work?"

"I'm assistant to the ambassador. I work closely with all the top-level people in the embassy and in the Crimean government. And I'm getting an education and experience that I could never have dreamed of a few years ago."

"Sounds like the Lord's been good to you."

A shadow passed over Victoria that was instantaneous and barely perceptible, but Paladin noticed it. But in a millisecond she was vibrant again. "Keller says I'm a natural," she beamed. "And he's promised that as he moves up, he'll take me along with him."

Paladin felt a tinge of a chill overwhelm him. He'd never felt anything like it. He couldn't even mask it. Victoria paused. "What's wrong, Brother Smith?"

"Oh, nothing," he explained. "Just a little headache. I'm fine."

"I'm sorry," she sympathized. "Are you okay?"

The chill passed. "I'm fine, really. I want to hear more. You seem to be going places."

"Ian, that's the ambassador, says there are opportunities opening up for us, even in a time of crisis. Oh, you've got to meet him. He's incredible." Her face brightened another level. "What are you doing right now?"

"Now?" he parried. "I just flew in. I'm exhausted."

"Oh, come on. The night is young," she coaxed. "Listen, Ian's just getting back from a short flight to Ukraine tonight. I promised I'd meet him for a late dinner at nine. Come with me."

"I'd be intruding."

"No, you wouldn't. How often do I find an old friend in the ballroom at the Hotel Crimea? Besides he's such a gentleman. And he'd be delighted to greet another American. Please, Brother Smith?" Her eyes danced.

There was plenty of time for introductions. And he *was* tired. He was as reluctant to meet Ian Keller as he had been to enter the Caucasus Room. But again something inside him told him it would be wise to go and go now. He smiled.

"All right. Let's go. But none of that Brother Smith stuff, Toria. It's Paladin now."

*Toria.* He'd never called her that before. It felt instinctive tonight. It's what her friends used to call her.

Something else felt instinctive. There would be no coaxing Toria Grant onto a homeward bound airplane—at least not immediately. No, she'd found her dream in Crimea. This would take some convincing. If this were the Lord's errand, the Lord would have to show him the way.

# 5

## AMBASSADOR IAN KELLER

**T**HE TAXI PULLED up to the curb of the American Embassy, a well-lighted, gated, gray mansion fronted by Doric columns and two Marine guards. Situated in a nicer suburb of Rostov, it was removed from the garish neon lights and the blaring horns of the city. Toria hopped out and paid the driver, then waited for Paladin to come around to her.

She stood proudly and gestured with one hand. "Isn't it beautiful? I live here."

Paladin looked up at the stately manor admiringly. It *was* impressive. "I thought just the Ambassador . . ."

"Ian has suites here for me and his secretary, Jeffries. We work very closely with him, especially right now. Come on in."

They walked up the steps to a gate where the Marines waited for her to identify herself and her guest. After they examined Paladin and his identification, he followed her into a large entryway showcased by a magnificent chandelier and a huge spiral staircase that wove around the edge of the room to the second story.

Paladin couldn't help himself as his eyes followed the rise of the curving staircase. But at the top step his gaze froze. There at the railing stood a man, impeccably dressed for the evening, in a suit and tie—Ian Keller. Paladin's face must have registered mild surprise because Keller seemed amused, but not the least bit curious for the moment.

"Victoria," he said as he started down the stairs. "I've been here for ten minutes. You know how I hate to be kept waiting."

He was smiling, but there was a certain serious edge to his playfulness. She met him at the bottom of the stairs, and he gave her a continental style kiss on the cheek. It suited him. It was the kind of greeting he would give. But the familiarity of it bothered Paladin.

"Where have you been?" Without waiting for an answer he looked over her head and finally acknowledged Paladin. "And did you bring home a stray?"

"Ian, I was dancing in the Hotel Crimea, and I happened to meet my old teacher, Mr. Paladin Smith. I might have even mentioned him to you before."

"I don't recall." He stepped over to Paladin and extended his hand. "Very nice to meet you, Mr. Smith. You are an American, then?"

"Yes, sir." Paladin retracted his hand from Keller's grip and rubbed his fingers together. He didn't like the *feel* of that handshake.

Keller took no notice. He'd already turned to his secretary, a gaunt man with a toad-like expression, who stood off to the side of the room. "Jeffries, ask the maid to put on another plate for dinner, would you?" He turned back to Paladin. "It's a very light meal considering the hour, but would you be our guest?"

—

Dinner at the American Embassy was hardly a light meal. It consisted of four courses: a small salad with vinegar dressing, a light borscht-like soup, and a main dish of chicken breast in white

58

sauce with asparagus, followed by a dessert of cheesecake and raspberry topping. It was absolutely a dream meal considering he had begun this long day eating Russian airline food.

They ate at the end of a long table—Ian Keller at the head, with Toria and Paladin on each side of him. Jeffries had eaten earlier but was still not far away, almost like a servant in waiting, in case he was needed. In that tight triangle, the conversation ebbed and flowed in the direction of the host of the embassy. He was a man who enjoyed being in control of every element of his life.

"So, Mr. Smith, what part of the United States are you from?"

"Well, I was born in California," Paladin explained. "But I've wandered around the country so much I think I qualify as a proud resident of America."

"Ha!" Keller laughed and congratulated Paladin. "Very good, very good. And exactly how are you and Victoria acquainted?"

The perfect ringmaster, Keller was determined to know everything. "I was just one of Toria's teachers in high school."

"Hmm," he acknowledged, "and I'm sure Victoria was a fine student."

Toria smiled. "That's because Brother Smith . . . I mean, Paladin was an excellent teacher."

"Paladin," Keller continued as he resumed his meal. "That's an unusual name—Paladin. Where did it come from?"

"Well," began Smith, looking at Toria, "my father grew up in the '40s and '50s. His favorite TV show was a western called 'Have Gun Will Travel.'"

"Ah, yes, yes, yes," reflected the ambassador. "The San Francisco gunslinger—a man in black who righted the wrongs of the defenseless." Paladin was impressed. Ian Keller was certainly charming and intelligent. "And so he named you after his hero. Tell me, Mr. Smith, do you carry a hair-trigger Colt .45 like Richard Boone?"

"No," Paladin apologized. "I don't care very much for guns, and

I'm not a real fan of violence. There are other differences between us too. *That* Paladin didn't teach religion and never wore a scarf."

"Mmm," acknowledged Keller with a bland smile. "Right now, this poor country is very much about guns and violence, isn't it, Victoria?"

"Exactly what *is* going on in Crimea?" asked Paladin.

"Oh, everything you've already read about in the newspapers. Russia is engaged in military exercises to the north. That activity worries members of Parliament, who fear the Russians are their enemies. Parliament argues with the prince and the nobility who feel the Russians are their friends. The people, anxious over hard times, follow the impulse of their leaders and also argue over the depths of the crisis. University students stage sit-ins and protests. Labor unions go on strike. Everybody wants to be part of something going on. And so the military must be called on to restore order. Then the Russians, in good faith, offer their military strength in support of a neighbor against civil anarchy. And the entire cycle starts over again in an ever-deepening rut. It's actually all very simple."

Keller had certainly summarized the situation perfectly. By his explanation every thread of the unraveling fabric was neatly wrapped into one tight ball of twine.

"So," probed Paladin, "you think the Russian presence is as easily and harmlessly explained as that?"

"Oh, yes," condescended Keller, "unless you're one of those insufferable 'Russophobes' who believe the former Soviets are responsible for every evil in Eastern Europe."

Keller laughed delightedly at the thought of anyone being so stupid as to disagree with him. But Paladin sensed that it was all part of a professional performance. This was the delicate science of diplomacy that the ambassador had mastered into an art form.

Paladin watched Keller ply his trade while he himself dutifully filled his role as audience and straight man, depending on the need. Meanwhile the adoring crowd sat directly across the table.

Toria studied Keller with fascination and hung on every word. She was still a student, and Ian Keller was her mentor.

But there was more. It wasn't romance, but Paladin sensed something wrong about Keller and his relationship with Toria Grant. He couldn't put his finger on it. She might not even be aware of it. But there was something more, and it was dark.

As they neared the end of the meal, Paladin was satisfied that he'd carefully played answer man to Keller's game of twenty questions. He also sensed that Keller too was satisfied, but not finished. Straightening himself from the table, he surveyed his surroundings and made his next probing move. "Victoria!" he remarked with calculated concern. "You haven't had a sip of wine this evening.[6] Are you feeling well?"

Toria looked down at her plate and then at Keller. Her voice was barely above a whisper. "I'm fine, Ian. I just don't feel like it tonight." She smiled at him, but there was no luster behind it.

Keller looked at her for a moment and then without moving his head, his eyes darted across the table to Paladin. Paladin barely saw the maneuver as he reached for his own water glass. This man was toying with his dinner companions, like a spider playing with flies. He enjoyed the sport. And he scored points by avoiding detection. Paladin was tired of this entertainment. He wondered if it were possible to throw Keller off balance.

"Well, I'll tell you," Paladin interrupted the awkwardness, "I could sure use something to drink."

Keller reached for the wine bottle. "Certainly, Mr. Smith—"

Paladin cut him off politely but instantly. "No, thank you, not that. Is this really all you have to drink at the American Embassy—wine and water? Don't you people ever drink anything (hic!) unfermented?" He laughed to himself. Keller didn't. "No, really, Ambassador. You must have some nectars, juices,

6. The Latter-day Saint law of health, the Word of Wisdom, emphasizes the proper care of the body and specifically prohibits the use of alcohol, tobacco, coffee, black tea, and illegal drugs.

fruit of the vine—cherry, grape, apple." He paused a beat. "You do, don't you?"

Paladin looked at his hosts. Toria was wide-eyed with surprise. Keller stared at Paladin with his mouth half open in uncharacteristic shock. Any embarrassment intended for Toria a moment before was totally forgotten.

"I'm sorry," stuttered Paladin in mock retreat. "Is there something wrong with the juice in Eastern Europe?"

"Jeffries?" ordered Keller, controlling himself. "Ask the maid to bring Mr. Smith a tall glass of cherry juice." There was a pause. "Jeffries!"

"Yes, sir." Paladin heard a weak voice squeak behind him before footsteps left the room.

"Thank you, Ambassador," Paladin said graciously. "And, please, call me Paladin."

Paladin had no idea how much of a professional he was dealing with. Keller took a cleansing breath and regrouped instantly. "Well . . . Paladin. It has been a perfectly delightful evening. And it has been wonderful to meet someone whom Victoria so respects."

He stood from the table and looked at his watch. "Unfortunately I'm afraid I've spent the entire evening getting acquainted when you two might have had the opportunity to catch up on old times."

"That's quite all right," Paladin followed his example. "I just arrived this afternoon. We'll have plenty of time for that."

Keller looked suddenly surprised. "Victoria, didn't you tell him?"

Toria, who was now standing, looked momentarily clueless. Then, all at once, the light dawned in. "Oh, my gosh, Ian. In all the excitement I completely forgot."

"Forgot what?" Paladin glanced from one of them to the other.

"We'll be flying to Moscow on Friday for several days," explained the ambassador with a condescending smile. "A diplomatic conference."

Instantly Paladin felt the blood flow out of his face. He held onto the back of his chair to hold himself steady and blinked to keep his composure.

He had been watching Keller and was sure, not only that the ambassador noted the change, but also that the flash of a faint smile stole across his lips. The sport was still on, and Keller was enjoying it. But far more than that, there was doom in the ambassador's announcement, and something deep inside Paladin revolted at it. It was the strongest impression he had sensed all evening. He had *never* felt anything like it. This was no whispering of the Spirit. This was the jolt of an earthquake—a shouted command from the center of his soul.

*STOP THEM!*

Paladin was completely taken aback by the spiritual explosion. But Keller did not notice it. He was busy concluding his thought to Toria. "As a matter of fact, you and I will be in briefing most of tomorrow. We have a lot to prepare."

Paladin obeyed his spiritual impression instantly, without even forming a reasoned thought in his brain. "I'm afraid that won't be possible!" he blurted, cutting off Keller mid-sentence.

The dining room became absolutely silent. Keller and Toria both froze like statues as they stared at their guest in stunned disbelief. Keller's face registered the full spectrum of displeasure. He wasn't at all used to being spoken to like this.

Finally he moved and turned to Paladin. This time there was no manufactured charm in his manner.

"I beg your pardon." He glared at Paladin with a frown.

Now what? Paladin lived a thousand lifetimes in the tense seconds that followed—mostly because he had nothing to answer. *I'm afraid that won't be possible?* What a stupid thing to say. He had just challenged the most powerful American in Crimea in a card game where the deck was stacked. The ambassador was calling his idiotic bluff and he had nothing in his hand. Nothing!

It was time to retreat. Could he talk his way out of this? Maybe explain that what he really meant was . . . What *did* he really mean? What else *could* he have meant? Paladin began to laugh nervously and run his hands through his pockets, a habit of anxiety he'd had ever since he was a kid.

"Well, I, uh . . ." It was then that his hand felt it in his coat pocket. Why he'd even brought it with him on leaving his room at the hotel he didn't know. The letter! Of course. His face brightened. The laughter and the nervousness were gone. He drew it out and faced the ambassador squarely. And Keller, recognizing strength in the visitor, withdrew, if only an inch.

Keller looked suspiciously at the envelope as Paladin handed it to him. "This letter will explain everything," said Paladin. Then he waited.

Keller leered at Paladin, then opened the letter and read.

> *To whom it may concern,*
>
> *This letter is to present Mr. Paladin Smith to United States Ambassador Ian Keller at the American Embassy in Rostov, Crimea. Mr. Smith will explain his business with you upon his arrival.*
>
> *(signed)*
> *Philip Chase*
> *House of Representatives*
> *United States of America*

The ambassador was calm when he finished the letter. He refused to react. His face was stoic. No one could guess what thoughts went on behind those calculating eyes as they looked at Paladin emotionlessly. Without a glance in her direction he handed the unfolded letter to Toria.

"What have you brought me, Victoria?" he asked blandly.

Toria took the letter and read it hungrily, her eyes growing wider with each word. Then she lowered the letter and looked with dismay at the man who had presented it. "I'm sure I don't know, Ambassador."

Keller's eyes were steel bullets now. "What is the meaning of this, Mr. Smith?"

Indeed, what *was* the meaning of this? Again Paladin had no idea how to respond. He hadn't considered a single thought beyond this point. This was all improvisation. But he *was* in control. Still, that was of little use if he didn't keep charging forward—somewhere.

"Perhaps we can discuss it tomorrow," he said. "The nature of my mission is confidential."

"Pardon me," countered Keller, "but the nature of your mission seems to be official."

"Then let us call it officially confidential." Paladin hoped that had sounded diplomatic, though perfectly evasive. He glanced at Toria, who was staring at him with her mouth open.

"Well," Keller stepped in. His voice was strangely resigned to the situation. It was as if he'd totally recalibrated his mind to an awkward reality. "We can't very well have you sleeping in a hotel downtown at any rate. You should move to the embassy first thing in the morning. Then we can conduct your business more conveniently. Would that meet with your approval, Mr. Smith?"

"That would be fine," said Paladin.

"Then, tomorrow," Keller said, settling the matter. "Victoria, why don't you send an official car for Mr. Smith in the morning—to relocate him to the embassy? In fact, you might even escort him. Is that to your liking, Mr. Smith?"

"Yes, I'll be ready at eight."

"Good," seethed Toria, "I'll be there at ten." With a glare that was homicidal she turned on her heels and left the room.

"Well then," said Keller with a patronizing smile, "there it is."

Paladin stood uncomfortably. Jeffries cleared his throat from the doorway. "There is a taxi waiting for you at the main entry, Mr. Smith." That was definitely his cue—a "Here's your hat. What's your hurry?" kind of an invitation. Paladin took a brief, awkward bow and left the room accompanied by a waiting Marine corporal. Jeffries closed the door behind him.

—

It was perfectly quiet in the dining room as Keller stood in place, collecting his thoughts.

Jeffries finally spoke. "Who is he, Ambassador?"

"I don't know," Keller answered with controlled calmness.

"What do you suppose he wants?"

"I don't know." There was the slightest edge to his voice.

"And why is here *now*?"

"I DON'T KNOW!" he shouted in an outburst of rage. Jeffries flinched, but Keller immediately composed himself. He was trying to piece this together. "An obscure member of the House of Foreign Affairs Committee sends this unknown messenger with a mysterious task that he obviously wants to handle in secrecy. Do you suppose this Congressman Chase knows something?"

"How could he, Ambassador?'

"Yes, how could he?" He was thinking. "And we're certainly not going to muddy the water trying to find out what he does know." Then he addressed Jeffries. "We've got to be very cautious—especially now. We're going to have to cancel our departure for Moscow. Meanwhile, let's show Mr. Smith every deference. Quietly attach him to the embassy. Give him reasonable clearance and allow him to harmlessly snoop around." Then he added as an afterthought. "And ask our friends to find out what they can about him."

"But what will we *do* with him in the meantime?"

"We follow the counsel of Machiavelli—Keep your friends close, your enemies closer, and if any mysterious visitors pay a visit, don't take your eyes off them."

# 6

## THE WHITE CATHEDRAL

A FTER A GOOD night's sleep, Paladin woke up amazingly refreshed. He cleaned up, prayed, and, even before breakfast, patched onto the hotel Internet to send an email.

*Dear Rachel,*

*You wouldn't believe the last several hours of my life. Since my arrival in Crimea, I have barely had time to stop. The Lord has had things for me to do. Miracles have taken place. And the impossible has already been made possible—many times. I found Victoria Grant last night—my first night here. I also met Ian Keller. Anything we thought we knew about Keller has been grossly underestimated. There is darkness there. And there is a reason I am here. What it is we shall see.*

*Give my best to Dad. And please give him a message with regards to the workings of the Spirit. (1 Kings 19:11–12) Usually the Lord is indeed a "still small voice." But on rare occasions he* ***is*** *in "the wind . . . the earthquake. . . and the fire."*

*I love you, and I miss you. I so wish you were here to give my life stability in the midst of the chaos that is surrounding me—and growing.*

*Love,*

*Paladin*

He then returned to his room to gather his few things and prepared to check out. He also had to consider his course of action for the day, and the next few days.

He was uncertain what Toria's attitude would be toward him when she arrived to escort him to the embassy. He didn't expect it to be pleasant. The young woman who left the embassy dining room last night was not happy.

One thing was for sure. He couldn't tell her why he'd really come to Crimea. Not now. Not only would it sound ridiculous— "I've come to rescue you"—but it would undermine his justification for being in the embassy, and for demanding that she and Keller remain in the country. No, the die was cast. He'd just have to play it out.

As far as today was concerned, he couldn't for the life of him think of a single direction he should go in. *Is this how Nephi felt?* For the last half hour before Toria's scheduled arrival, he settled into his normal routine of prayer and scripture study, although it was difficult for him to keep his mind focused. If he was going to keep up this bluff today, he needed to get an inkling from the Lord of what the bluff was. He still felt very much in the dark.

At 10:00 a.m. a knock on the door of his hotel room interrupted his reading. He stood, swallowed, and, stepping to the door, opened it.

Toria stood there alone, her entire body telegraphing an attitude of quiet contempt. Her face was the expression of anger itself. But Paladin didn't have to rely on body language or facial features to interpret her. She spoke immediately.

"Let's go." Her voice was icy, and her eyes were lifeless. She turned and walked resolutely to the elevator. With his arms full, Paladin struggled to catch up with her. She'd pressed the button for the lobby already, and he barely made it inside before the doors closed.

They exited the elevator and checked out of the hotel without a word. Toria waited for him to complete his business at the main desk, then led him quickly from the lobby and through the hotel's double glass doors to a waiting limousine. It was all Paladin could do to keep up with her.

She climbed into the backseat and slammed the door while the embassy driver got out to place Paladin's luggage into the trunk. Then Paladin took his own seat in the back of the car, and they pulled away. Still, Toria hadn't said a word since they left his room.

It was a few minutes later when Toria finally spoke, but not to Paladin. In crystal clear Russian, she conversed with the driver. He said something back as he nodded. The car turned at the next corner and all was silent again until they came to a stop at the curb of a green expanse marked with trees, flowers, and walkways.

"Where are we?" asked Paladin.

"Memorial Gardens," she said matter-of-factly as she got out of the car. "We're sightseeing."

Paladin scrambled out of the car and caught up with her on the main walkway. "What happened to the embassy?"

"I have an assignment from Ambassador Keller," Toria spoke without looking at him. "I'm to try and find out what you're about before I bring you back. I suppose because I'm responsible for loosing you on him, I should be responsible for explaining you to him."

"Oh, Toria," he reasoned. "Keller can't really blame *you* for my presence here."

"I don't know if he does or not. But frankly, why shouldn't he? I took you to him as a friend of mine, innocent as a lamb, and then you turned on him like a predator. You used me and then you betrayed me—for the second time in my life."

Paladin froze in his steps as Toria walked on ahead. He was speechless. Rachel was right after all. This was a woman's scorn— the wrath of a woman suddenly *twice* wronged.

Toria was ten paces ahead of him before he had the presence of mind to follow her. But before he had taken one stride, she turned angrily on her heels, faced him, and shouted, practically in tears, "I've never been so humiliated by anyone . . . ever!"

People in the park were turning curiously to stare at the two of them, though they could not understand a word of her English outcries.

Paladin tried to calm her. "Toria, it was never my intention to embarrass you. I didn't expect to confront Keller last night. And I didn't ever *plan* to use that letter."

"Who are you?" she demanded. "I thought you were a seminary teacher."

"Actually, I'm a history teacher."

"Right! With a diplomatic letter of introduction from my uncle, Congressman Philip Chase, to the ambassador, which implies that some kind of informal investigation is about to take place—conducted by you. Why are you here? What are you up to?"

Paladin figured he'd been patient enough. He finally let go. "Me? What is *your ambassador* up to?"

Toria reacted with the defensiveness of a mother bear. "*He* is looking out for the best interests of the United States of America on foreign soil. You've got a lot of nerve to question his intentions or his integrity."

"Integrity?" Paladin lashed out. "Exactly what do you know about Ian Keller?"

"Apparently more than I know about you," she countered. "Starting with fifteen years of distinguished service in diplomacy and a reputation as a dedicated American citizen."

"Toria, Ian Keller is nothing but a 2.0 version of Jace Packard."

Toria was suddenly livid. "How dare you throw that in my face! And how dare you compare Ian to that teenage rapist, especially after Ambassador Keller has been so good to me!"

"I saw how good he was to you," Paladin came back. "Keller is a manipulative reptile. He twisted and turned his way around that dinner conversation like a python—and then chose just the right moment to *truly* humiliate you. And he knew exactly what he was doing. That is *not* a good man."

"Is this about the wine?" she asked incredulously. "Well, perhaps my life has changed a little bit since I left seminary and BYU. Maybe the world I live and work in just isn't up to your standards."

"Those weren't my standards on display last night. They were yours." She bit her lip angrily, but said nothing. "Besides, we're not talking about you or me. We're talking about the all-controlling, all-observant Ian Keller. Did you notice how he called all the shots, asked all the questions? We found out everything there is to know about me last night and learned nothing about him."

"My original point," she answered. "As of last night I don't think we *do* know anything about you. Who are you, Brother Smith, and who do you work for?"

Paladin smiled in spite of the intensity of the conversation. "Brother Smith" sounded so comical under the circumstances. "Just Paladin, please."

"Oh, then please, *Paladin* or whoever you are—because I'm not sure who you are, or what are you doing here. Who sent you?"

"Your uncle."

"My uncle hasn't got the brains that God gave a soda cracker, and you know it."

Paladin subdued a chuckle. Yes, that was Chase all right. "Are you accusing your uncle of being stupid?"

"Of course I am. He's a congressman." Toria squinted her eyes at Paladin. "Uncle Philip is just fronting for the committee or someone else—someone higher. I want to know who."

Paladin shrugged in resignation. "You wouldn't believe it."

"Try me," she parried. "Somebody powerful enough to move the machinery, who thinks they've got all the information on Crimea, and the right to meddle in diplomatic affairs."

Paladin considered. "Well, that's pretty much it."

"And what makes you think your information is good?"

"Actually," Paladin replied, "my sources are very classified and extremely reliable."

Toria stared at him for a moment and shook her head. "You might think you can play this game with me. But Ian Keller isn't to be trifled with like some teenager."

There was a long silence again. When Paladin spoke his words were measured. "I have never trifled with you."

Toria smiled ruefully and began walking again under the shadow of a war memorial. "Your performance, past or present, doesn't bear that out."

"Do we have to keep going back to high school?" asked Paladin.

"Yes, we do." Toria turned on him angrily—almost hysterically. "Because you apparently had no idea how difficult my life was."

"Toria, I knew what you were going through."

"Oh, I thought you understood," she said, holding back her tears. "I was thrown into Orange County—an orphan—absolutely adrift. Without parents, without friends. I'd lost everything—even my faith in God. And then there *you* were—this awesome teacher who gave me hope and something to get up for and look forward to every day. I saw something in you. I looked up to you. And then on that horrible night, when I called, you came." She paused. "You don't realize what that meant to me. Did you know you were the only real friend I had? The only person in my life who I felt cared about me? And then, just like everybody else who meant anything to me, you suddenly ceased to exist one day. Zap! No explanations. No good-byes. You might as well have gotten killed in a wreck just like my parents. You just died. And part of me died all over again."

She sniffed back the tears. "And now after seven years you pop up in Crimea. But it's not even you. It's some specter on a secret mission that I'm afraid is going to hurt me again." She turned to walk away.

Stopping her, Paladin held her by the shoulders and turned her toward him. "Wait! Didn't your uncle ever tell you why I stopped teaching? Why I left? Didn't anybody?"

"No, you just vanished. What did it have to do with Uncle Phil?"

Paladin's eyes wandered from her face as he considered everything Toria never knew. "Nothing. It was apparently a pretty well-kept secret."

"You have a lot of those," she said, still not comprehending.

Paladin was blunt. "You really have no idea."

She shook her head slightly in bewilderment.

"Chase and Old Man Packard—they pressed charges and threatened to prosecute. Your uncle resented the attention I was giving you in the first place—you know, the sporting events, the concerts. He thought you were falling in love with me."

Toria looked away, and her faced flushed red. She smiled, but it disappeared instantly. "My stupid uncle," she said in a whisper and bit her lip. "That's ridiculous."

Paladin raised an eyebrow, but she didn't see it. He continued. "That's what I told him. Ridiculous." Paladin walked on.

This time Toria caught up. "Why so ridiculous?"

"Oh, you know, a pretty teenage girl like you and an old guy like me—and your teacher too," he explained.

"Well, yeah," she conceded, "I see what you mean."

Paladin looked over at her. "Why are you blushing?"

"I . . . I'm not blushing," she said, looking away. "I'm just cold." They walked again in silence for a few paces. "Well, what happened?"

"What happened?" Paladin erupted. "Your dear uncle Phil rode me out of town on a rail. I quit the only job I ever loved and left Southern California. I thought it was best if I slipped away quietly. Less embarrassing for everybody . . . especially you. It was that simple."

Toria was silent for a few paces. "I'm sorry, Brother Smith. I never knew."

"Call me Paladin."

"What happened then?"

Paladin chuckled to himself. "I joined the army."

"You're kidding!"

"No." He smiled and shook his head. "Of course, they discharged me as soon as they found out about a closed head injury I had as a baby. Car accident. Craniotomy. I tell ya, sometimes your parents do spoil everything."

Toria smirked. "Yeah. Tell me about it."

They came to a bench in the park, and he motioned for her to sit. She did without resistance, and he sat beside her a few inches away.

"At that point I became a bum—a card-carrying tramp. I just wandered around the country for a couple of years, searching for myself, working here and there. I returned to California when my mother died. That's when I met Rachel—and stopped wandering. If it hadn't been for her, and the direction she gave my life, I'd still be a hobo. Instead, I settled down and got purpose. I worked for a while in advertising. Then finally I got back into teaching. And that's my life to the present."

Toria had listened calmly, without judgment. "That doesn't explain your presence here."

"You've got to trust me," he said. "Please, be patient."

Without responding she looked off, stood again, and took his hand. "Come with me," she said, the tone of her voice lifting. "I want to show you something I think you'll like."

Toria led him a short distance through an avenue of birch trees that were changing colors and losing their leaves.

When she stopped, they stood before a large pool of shallow water. There, reflecting on its surface, perhaps a thousand yards away towered a magnificent Byzantine temple—sparkling white and beautiful against the brilliant blue sky, topped with a huge golden dome and framed by four smaller cupolas.

Paladin stood silent and reverent before the pool as he took it in. Toria gazed expectantly at the cathedral and then at him. "Can we go inside?" he asked and glanced at her. Without a word she smiled and nodded. Her eyes danced again as she led the way around the pool to the walkway that led toward the cathedral.

They didn't speak as they made their way to the structure and fell under its massive shadow.

Paladin finally broke the silence with a whisper. "What is it?" he asked in total awe.

"This is the Russian Orthodox Cathedral of the Resurrection," she answered quietly with equal veneration. "Isn't it beautiful?"

They passed through the gargantuan doors of the public church and found themselves in a museum dedicated to the soul. Icons and statuary ornamented every nook, ceiling, and pillar. Tapestries and paintings hung on every wall. And candles and incense touched the unconscious sensations. Toria removed a small pamphlet from a wooden box at the door and handed it to Paladin. He graciously took and opened it, then smiled. "I don't understand Russian." He shrugged helplessly.

Taking the pamphlet she cleared her throat and began to translate. "The original white Cathedral of the Resurrection—"

"Shh," came a voice from behind them. It was one of the unofficial Russian Orthodox "guards" on duty to enforce reverence.

Toria glanced in the direction of the complaint, and then at Paladin as she came closer to try again, lowering her voice to an undertone. "The original white Cathedral of the Resurrection was constructed by King Gregory of Crimea to celebrate the retreat of Napoleon from Russia in 1840. Taking over ten years to build, it occupied this site for over one hundred years. Then in 1951, as part of a religious purge, the Communist government of Russia had the cathedral's art treasures removed and the sacred structure razed to the ground. The Church in Crimea was expected to disappear with it."

She stopped reading and looked up at him expectantly. Her eyes fairly sparkled again.

"This ought to be a great ending," Paladin whispered. "Obviously the Orthodox Church is still here and"—he shifted his eyes to the ceiling—"so is the cathedral. What did they do? Hide it piece by piece?"

"No," she said patiently, "the Russians destroyed the cathedral all right. But the Orthodox Church grew stronger."

Paladin grinned knowingly. "That's the way it always works."

Toria read again in a soft voice. "Following *perestroika* and Crimea's breakaway from the Soviet Union, the foundations for the restored Cathedral of the Resurrection were laid on the site of the original landmark. After several years the painstaking duplicate was finally completed with the opening of the new century—a symbol of the future of the nation and their soul."

Toria closed the pamphlet and tucked it into the inside pocket of Paladin's jacket. "This cathedral represents the people of Crimea. They're good people, Paladin. They're struggling right now. And their national future may be in the balance. Promise me you didn't come to hurt them. Promise me you came to help."

Paladin looked at her for a long moment. When he spoke, his answer surprised him. "I promise."

Just then the bells in the huge dome chimed, making a soft, rich, and powerful tone that carried throughout the white temple. Toria looked up and then around her, totally wrapped in the wealth of sound, which seemed to engulf eternity. She still gazed upward as she spoke. "What is it I feel here?"

Paladin inhaled deeply and smiled with satisfaction. "It's the Savior." Her eyes connected with his thoughtfully and then drifted away as she turned and walked through the cavernous interior filled with crosses and Madonnas. Paladin casually followed her. When she reached a corner out of the way of the worshippers, she spoke again without facing him.

"Paladin, about the wine—"

"Toria, you don't have to explain anything to me."

"No, I want to say something. You . . . you're really still so very much the same guy who taught me in seminary. But I'm different. I've changed. I'm not the same wide-eyed teenager who used to sit in your early-morning class. Part of me moved on over the past seven years. Part of me got left behind. I don't know if that part will ever come back again. I don't know if it's meant to."

"That's what the Communists would have said about this cathedral." He paused, and she turned to look at him. He continued, "But it's here."

She half smiled and cocked her head. "Yep," she looked around. "It's here."

"Toria," asked Paladin, "do you still have your patriarchal blessing?"[7]

Toria started walking back around the periphery of the cathedral. Paladin stepped in beside her. "No. I didn't bring any of that stuff with me. It's all part of that life I left behind." She spoke without so much as a glance at him.

From a distant open chapel of the huge enclosure, a small choir of monks began to sing a capella. Their voices blended perfectly, filling the cathedral with the harmonious sounds of heaven.

Toria stopped and listened intently while her eyes seemed to search the air before she closed them. Paladin watched her and then breathed in the atmosphere one last time.

She opened her eyes and looked at him. "We probably ought to be getting back to the embassy."

Paladin nodded. "Toria, I'm sorry I wasn't able to share more with you."

She smiled and squeezed his arm. "Don't apologize. You shared more than you'll ever know."

---

7. A patriarchal blessing is a special ordinance administered by an ordained patriarch (an office of the higher or Melchizedek Priesthood). Available to every worthy, baptized member of the church, it is most frequently given to young people. The patriarchal blessing is considered to be a personal, inspired statement of direction and counsel from the Lord.

# 7

# A Royal Invitation

Ian Keller sat in his spacious office at the American Embassy smoking a cigarette as he studied a document he had received only a short time ago. His brows were uncharacteristically creased with worry. He was too intent on his task to be startled when there was a knock at the door.

"Come in."

Jeffries entered and immediately began to talk as he crossed the room to the huge desk. "I have a preliminary report on Mr. Paladin Smith." A nod from Keller indicated that he should continue. "He arrived yesterday on an Aeroflot flight non-stop from Los Angeles. Came straight to the Crimean where he made contact with Ms. Grant. No indication that she has any complicity with him or Congressman Chase. In less than twenty-four hours his activities have been very limited so far."

Jeffries leafed to a second sheet of paper and continued. "In our favor, he doesn't seem to understand a word of Russian. The taxi driver who brought him from the airport and the staff at the hotel are sure of it. They're convinced he's just a pleasant, stupid American. Other than that I'm afraid there's not much information on him yet."

"How can that be? There has to be some diplomatic background."

"Nothing, sir. The man is a blank slate. Listed in our *Who's Who* as a history teacher in Southern California. Nothing remarkable or suspicious at face value except his enlistment in the military and application to the Special Forces. Then he suddenly drops off the radar for two years."

Keller pursed his lips and leaned back. "That's noteworthy. But hardly worth worrying about on the face of it. Nothing more than a blundering teacher on vacation." He tapped the document on his desk in front of him. "You've seen this?"

"Yes," confirmed Jeffries. "The email he sent from the hotel this morning, supposedly to his wife in California. It's all very cryptic. We can't make heads or tails out of it."

The ambassador picked up the email again and looked it over. "Acknowledgment of a mission, specific uncomplimentary references to me, scriptural notations, and a request to relay a message to some higher authority."

"Do you suppose it's some kind of code?" asked Jeffries.

"Could be. Still, it doesn't fit." Keller carefully filed the letter in a drawer at his desk and closed it. "For the time being we know what we need to know. I don't intend to let Mr. Smith on too long of a leash."

At that moment the intercom on Keller's telephone sounded with a soft buzz. "Yes, Ms. Sanders?"

Keller's secretary had been trained to follow directions specifically and efficiently. "Mr. Keller, you asked to be informed as soon as Ms. Grant and her American friend returned to the embassy."

"Thank you, Ms. Sanders." Keller quickly looked at his watch and stood from the desk. "I'll need to arrange things for this evening. Meanwhile, give Mr. Smith a tour of the embassy, answer questions, and keep him occupied for the afternoon. I want to postpone our meeting or any other direct confrontation with our guest until I can find out more about him."

"Then you've decided what to do with him?"

"Yes," answered Keller. "Whoever sent Smith made a poor choice in the hopes of keeping a low profile. But he's a rank amateur—way out of his league. So let's act before he does. Overwhelm him. Draw him out. See if we can get him to play his hand."

Composing himself and straightening his tie, Keller walked around his desk and past Jeffries to the door. He paused only briefly before opening it and stepping into the entryway where Toria and Paladin were approaching. He had timed his greeting perfectly.

"Victoria, my dear, good morning." He kissed her as he had the night before. "Mr. Smith."

"Paladin, please."

"Yes, of course. How was your morning? I thought you might enjoy a relaxing walk before you began the drudgery of your day here. Rostov is actually a beautiful city."

"It certainly is," agreed Paladin, politely.

"You arrived just in time for lunch," the ambassador graciously explained. "Then Jeffries will answer whatever questions you have regarding the embassy before you and I have our interview—later today or tomorrow."

Paladin was winging it again. "Uh, that would be just great."

"Although we may not have a chance today, frankly," said the ambassador, quite pleased with what he was about to announce. "We've been invited to the Royal Palace this evening to dine with the prince."

The reaction in the room was instantaneous. Victoria's eyes darted from the ambassador to Paladin, then fell to the floor with an expression of discomfort. Jeffries's face registered unconcealed worry. And Keller surveyed all of them with a subtle sweep of his vision and a bland, self-satisfied smile.

Paladin noticed all these subtleties, though he couldn't understand why he was sensitive to them or why they were important.

Toria was the first to speak. "Ian, must I go? I'm really not feeling very well."

"My dear Victoria, I'm afraid the prince would be very disappointed if you were not in attendance. Besides how could I present your friend without a proper introduction from you?"

Toria cast a knowing glance at Paladin. "I'm not really sure Paladin needs me as a calling card any longer."

But Keller was insistent. "No, Victoria, I won't hear another word of it. This is a professional duty. And the evening would be dramatically dull without you. Don't you agree, Mr. Smith?"

Paladin was loath to agree with Keller, but even more reluctant to let Toria out of his sight for the evening. He took a chance of upsetting her again. "Toria, I'd feel much better if you were there. I'm a little uncomfortable meeting a prince. Could you try?"

She gave him a look of exasperation that told him he might easily have crossed the line again. There was no way to find out for now.

"Then it's settled," Keller broke in. He took Toria by the arm and walked her to the spiral staircase. "I suggest you take the afternoon easy and rest for a few hours. I'll have lunch sent to your room. Relax until this evening. That ought to put a little color back in your cheeks. We'll meet you here at five o'clock and depart together for the palace. The dinner will be formal."

She stood at the bottom step and looked from Keller to Paladin. Then she smiled with resignation and shrugged. "Very well, Ian. Paladin."

—

Victoria turned and ascended the stairs to the second story, looking back to see Paladin watching her. She wondered now what he thought. She wondered what Ian thought. She *was* suddenly reluctant to visit the prince. His attentions to her had always been flattering and professionally helpful. The thought of his royal fawning only made her uncomfortable today.

She shook her head as she walked down the hallway. In all sincerity she *wasn't* feeling well. Maybe she *wouldn't* go. No, she had to.

She arrived at her room, went inside, and fell against the closed door in protected privacy. After a moment she turned and locked it with the key. She stood there for a moment, safe from any intrusion and stared at the vanity across the room. Walking quickly to it she sat and looked at herself for several seconds before scanning the drawers.

Taking a deep breath she began to open them one by one, peering inside and rummaging through their contents. In a few minutes the drawers were empty and the floor was littered with odds and ends, but as yet Toria had not found what she was searching for. It wasn't until she reached into the back of the bottom drawer that she found it—a weathered, dog-eared, and dust-covered copy of the Book of Mormon.

Taking the book, Toria wiped it off and held it in her hands—examining it as she turned it over once or twice. At length, she stood, walked over, and sat on the bed with the volume on her lap. She hadn't looked at this book for months. She certainly hadn't read it for years. It was, after all, nothing but a keepsake to her—a last remnant from her parents that she kept to remember them. She opened the front cover and read the inscription on the facing page.

> *To Toria,*
> *We're so proud of you for the decision you have made.*
> *On this, the day of your baptism,*
> *Love,*
> *Mom and Dad*

She closed her eyes and shut the book again. Why had she taken it out? It was better left in the back of the drawer. That was the past. She'd made other decisions now. Life had changed. Life was good, wasn't it?

She opened her eyes again and looked at the book. The gold letters of the title were blurred in her vision. She set the book beside her on the bed and shook her head.

Paladin Smith. What had he returned for? Why did he have to come back into her life? Things had been fine. They were still fine. But now . . .

Toria slowly looked over at the book again. She hadn't pulled it from the back of her vanity drawer to take a guilt trip down memory lane. She'd stopped going down that road a while ago. But something Paladin had said made her think. There was a part of her that had never been happy—a part that had always been missing. She'd never understood what it was. It seemed to call to her at the cathedral. And then Paladin reminded her in a single phrase where she might find it. It didn't make much sense. But she just wanted to look. There was nothing wrong with that.

She reached for the book again and, flipping it over, turned to the very end. There between the last page and the back cover, folded in quarters, she recognized what she was looking for and gingerly removed it. Carefully unfolding the paper, she spread it out on her lap—a legal-sized document, neatly typed on both sides. She eyed it from top to bottom and began to read.

*Victoria Rene Grant,*

*In the name of the Lord, Jesus Christ, and by the power and authority of the Holy Melchizedek Priesthood, I lay my hands upon your head and give unto you a patriarchal blessing . . .*

# 8

## PETER THE MEDIOCRE

**P**ALADIN SAT ALONE in the backseat of the embassy car as it wove its way through the streets of Rostov to the Royal Palace. The driver, a Crimean national employed by the diplomatic mission, spoke no English so the drive was quiet, leaving Paladin to his thoughts.

The afternoon had been a long one. Following a lunch of sumptuous food and uncomfortable conversation, he had been forced to endure a tour of the embassy conducted by Jeffries, who showed him every possible detail of diplomatic minutiae without introducing him to a single member of the embassy staff. Whether Jeffries was intentionally boring or was gifted with a particularly dull personality—Paladin had no idea. But he was seldom so glad to see a day come to a close in his life.

He retired to his room to find a tuxedo waiting for him—and it fit perfectly. His instructions were to meet Keller and Toria in the embassy entry at 5:00 p.m., and together they would depart for the palace. He did not think he could be disappointed *not* to find

Keller, but when Jeffries sat on the sofa waiting for him he feared the worst.

"They left without me?"

"They were forced to depart early at the request of Prince Peter," explained Jeffries. "Ms. Grant was particularly reluctant to leave without you, but it couldn't be helped. The prince felt it essential to be briefed on your mission before he received you."

Paladin looked at Jeffries for a moment in the chilling silence. "Of course," he said, "that will be difficult for them to share with him, won't it?"

"Since you haven't told them, yet," confirmed Jeffries. "Yes, I was going to mention that."

"Thank you," returned Paladin. "Is there anything I need to know about tonight before I go?"

"Only to be on your best behavior. You do represent the United States, and tonight's courtesy by the prince is a reception and dinner held in your honor."

"What?" gasped Paladin.

"Mr. Smith, you are a special envoy of the United States of America. The prince desires to welcome you as such. Now listen carefully. Your car is waiting. But there are certain protocols that must be observed when being received by foreign royalty."

At that point Jeffries condescendingly reviewed with Paladin how to approach and greet the prince as well as the other guests. Impatiently he had him practice it once, and then with a sigh and a shake of his head that said, "I guess that will have to do," he escorted Paladin out the door and into the waiting car.

They had been driving for several minutes now. The chauffeur said something in Russian as the vehicle slowed and turned at a grand entrance with a huge gate that opened before them. Continuing in the afternoon sunlight, the car curved its way along a cobbled driveway, edged with manicured lawns and sculptured rose gardens until it stopped in front of a set of broad marble steps.

Instantly Paladin's door opened. A uniformed page, standing straight as a picket and staring into the distance, waited for him to disembark. The driver motioned with his head to Paladin and Paladin responded, clambering out of the backseat. He stood, adjusted his tuxedo and his composure, and then looked to the page. But the man was not about to break character. Paladin looked around and found himself in front of nothing less than a structure built for a king. "So this is where the other half live."

A red carpet began at the bottom of the steps and ascended to the top of the broad stairway. There, two other pages waited, also dressed in royal uniform. This was obviously his engraved invitation.

Paladin slowly began to walk up the steps to the top of the stairway. Arriving, he looked ahead and saw that the red carpet proceeded to the double doors of the palace where two more pages stood, manning the entrance.

"I'll be awfully embarrassed if they're waiting for someone else," he muttered to himself and charged uncomfortably forward.

When he reached the entrance, the pages wordlessly reached over, pushed the double oak doors inward, and stood beside them. Paladin followed them as far as the threshold and froze—paralyzed both by what he saw and by what he heard.

His ears were greeted by the blare of royal trumpets, heralding his arrival. A room, full of formally attired guests in the midst of conversation, ceased their discussions and focused their attention on him.

"Mr. Paladin Smith, Special Envoy of the United States of America," boomed an echoing voice through the palace entry and hall. Instantly all the guests applauded.

Paladin smiled graciously, but in truth his feet were nailed to the floor. Had it not been for the page on his right he might have remained there all evening. "Walk toward the throne, sir," he whispered in a thick Russian accent.

Paladin nodded and forced himself to move. As he did he

allowed himself to look around the room. Never had he imagined himself walking in the midst of such splendor.

He watched his feet take their first steps on the enameled tiles of blue marble inlaid with regal crests. The floor was polished so perfectly it reflected the walls of the room like a lake—panel after panel of gold gilded grandeur, guarded by medieval statues of past Crimean kings who peered down on him disapprovingly. Stained glass windows high overhead permitted the waning afternoon light to dance off the gold leaf carvings of the ceiling, which stretched the entire length of the hall.

Paladin passed from the entry, beyond another two doors, and under a massive archway into a reception hall. This room, more brilliant and spacious than the first, was nothing less than a royal gallery. Glittering crystal chandeliers seemed to light every corner of the ornate chamber entirely of inlaid gold, jewels, and the minutest hand-painted detail. Framed artwork and tapestries decorated the upper walls throughout the gallery. And spanning the length of the room on either side of him were painted frescoes depicting heroic events from Crimean history.

Fascinated by the magnificence of his surroundings, Paladin turned his head in every direction as he stared with awe at the floors, the walls, and the ceiling. More than once in his procession through the huge rooms he rotated in a complete circle—as overwhelmed with the spectacle as a kid at a carnival and just as oblivious to the impression he might be making. He finally thrust his hands in his pockets and smiled to himself, completely consumed in the opulence of another world.

Not until then did he become aware of the other decoration in the gallery—the human gauntlet of the cream of Crimea, who had come to greet him, and who, at this point, were rather uncertain what to make of the American envoy.

Collecting himself to his full height of dignity, Paladin nodded to the lords and ladies on either side of him. Smiling, they nodded back. This was a good sign. *Keep walking*, he told himself. Walking where?

He looked to the front of the room. He'd been so preoccupied with the trappings of the gallery he had completely overlooked the centerpiece. The prince of Crimea waited, a mere twenty feet directly ahead of him. The sight was dazzling.

A golden archway, carved in the most intricate detail was set into the wall. Within the niche gleamed the most beautiful throne imaginable, gold and silver, encrusted with precious stones. And upon the royal chair sat Prince Pyotr of Crimea, dignified and regal, without a hint of levity on his neatly bearded face. He was not wearing the crown, but he was every inch the prince in dress and attitude.

To his left on the elevated throne platform stood Keller, looking disappointed in Paladin's entrance. On the prince's right, by contrast, stood Toria, who wore a barely suppressed grin that her sparkling eyes could not conceal for sheer mirth.

Paladin had come to himself just in time to recall the royal protocol Jeffries had so painstakingly taught him. He stopped short and stood motionless for a moment in thought. Then, bending low at the waist, he waited for another five seconds or so before straightening to his full height. He faced the prince in the silence, wondering if he had performed correctly, when, to his relief, the monarch smiled and nodded ever so slightly.

That was Paladin's signal to advance another several feet to the base of the steps ascending to the prince's throne. He did so and bowed low again before straightening. Now, if pleased, it was the prince's turn.

Paladin waited as the prince looked imperiously down upon him. Perhaps he wasn't pleased. How embarrassing would *that* be on the Crimean society page? Then, slowly the prince stood.

Without a glance at Paladin, he looked out over the assembled guests. "It is with pleasure," he announced in clear English with a slight Russian accent, "the Crown welcomes Mr. Paladin Smith, the Special Envoy of the United States, to the Royal Court of Crimea."

With that he extended his hand, which was the invitation for Paladin to ascend the throne steps, enter Peter's personal space, and take his royal hand. As he did so the prince's subjects acceded to his regal endorsement with universal applause. Keller begrudgingly nodded his approval. Toria beamed. So, this was diplomacy.

Prince Peter responded to the applause of the audience as though it were intended for him. Waving blandly to his guests he descended from the exalted throne and stepped down to the floor level, inviting Paladin to come with him. That of course was the cue of the reception invitees to come and greet the prince and to meet his special guest.

"Come, Mr. Smith," Peter invited, "I must present you to the nobility of Crimea."

Paladin followed with Keller and Toria immediately behind him. "Thank you, Your Majesty," he said. "I had no idea this was to be a state reception—in my honor."

Keller was quick to include himself in the conversation. "When the prince heard you had come as a special messenger, he insisted."

"The most influential people in Rostov are here tonight—just to meet you," added Toria.

"How in the world did you get them together on such short notice?" asked Paladin.

"I simply told them to come," explained the prince. "You in the West have such a difficult time understanding the concept of royalty and the voice of the king."

Paladin understood all right. There was a definite tone to the prince's voice that made him understand. Mere mortals were spoken down to here. That, he supposed, was the plight of the proletariat and the privilege of the prince in his own palace. Paladin was a lesser creature on these premises. But *all* of these people were lesser creatures. That was an unspoken, yet clear truth in the prince's world—together with another unstated reality: it was the prince's right to rule.

Paladin also quickly understood why the prince had been anxious to carefully stage this reception for him tonight. This reception was Prince Peter's opportunity to introduce *his* guest to *his* subjects, and he made the grandest show of it, as if Paladin were America's personal ambassador to him. And indeed Rostov's finest citizens were in attendance—religious leaders, military leaders, political leaders.

Among the most notable of these was Prime Minister Yuri Tiomkin, who looked exactly like the picture Paladin had been furnished by the State Department, right down to the gray hair and the red sash. Paladin wondered if he had any other clothes. It was already obvious that this country paid the royal family far more than it paid the parliament.

"Mr. Smith," said the statesman as he approached Paladin and bowed his head.

Paladin was surprised to hear clear English, though the Russian accent was more pronounced than that of the prince.

"Have you a moment?"

The two had been introduced moments before but now the crowd around Paladin had dissipated. Those few guests who were chatting with the visiting American politely excused themselves in deference to the prime minister, and he and Paladin were "alone" in the crowd.

Paladin could see Keller in a corner of the room observing this interview with a weather eye. It was becoming second nature to watch Keller watching him. But at present that wasn't his concern. "How may I help you, Mr. Prime Minister, I mean Your Excellency?"

"Please, Mr. Smith," Tiomkin waved him off, "you may dispense with all the formalities of state with which you are not accustomed."

*This man is no fool,* thought Paladin. "What do you mean?" he asked.

"It is obvious from your demonstrated 'mastery' of royal protocol that you are not a professional diplomat. That is no particular loss. But you are a representative of the United States on an official mission through your embassy to the Court of Crimea. As the leader of this government I am interested in your purpose here—especially at such a critical time in our history. A hostile force lurks on our borders. Internal powers plot with them for political favor. And our people are torn with anxiety and dread. Mr. Smith, we are in dire need of support from the West—from NATO, from America, and from your allies. It has not been forthcoming. If it fails to materialize, I don't know that we shall survive as a free people."

Paladin was dumbfounded that the Prime Minister should be confiding such things to him. Was the situation that desperate? "Mr. Tiomkin," he said in an undertone, "have you spoken to the ambassador as you have spoken to me?"

Tiomkin looked at Paladin as though he were child who had said something very naïve. "Mr. Smith, everyone knows Ambassador Keller is in the pocket of the prince."

"And the prince?" asked Paladin.

"The prince," whispered Tiomkin, "is in the pocket of Alexander Trotsky." The elder statesman shook his head in disappointment and began to turn away. "Thank you, Mr. Smith. But it doesn't appear that you can offer any assistance to us."

Paladin reached out and touched Tiomkin's arm before he had taken a step. "Your Excellency, if the West won't come to your aid—and they probably won't—can't your own people do something?"

Tiomkin's response was cold. "Against the Russians? I'm sorry I disturbed you," he said and walked off amid the other guests. Paladin watched him, somewhat haunted by the short conversation.

Suddenly he felt a nudge in his side. "Paladin." It was Toria. "I see you met the prime minister. What was he talking to you about?"

"Pockets," said Paladin, still following the path of the elder statesman. "Just pockets."

———

Dinner, held in the banquet hall, was an event such as Paladin had never been exposed to before. Seated at a table that seemed the length of a football field, the guests were treated to a seven-course meal of unrecognizable, though delicious, food.

Wine glasses were filled regularly with rare spirits by attentive servants and Paladin was vigilant to see that his was filled with apricot juice. He thought he noticed Toria ask for the same.

Across the table, just a few seats down, Paladin recognized a face he had not been introduced to at the reception—Colonel Dimitri Ustinov, head of the Crimean military.

No one could ever forget a face like that—mustached, hard, and cold. He was a bit older, a bit grayer, a bit more weathered than the photograph Paladin had become familiar with. But his was the face, and that was the frame—full, muscular, and perfectly erect. This man was born to command.

At the head of the table sat the prince. All the guests of rank sat near him, but none in any pattern of established position of recognition, with the exception of Toria, who was placed at his right hand.

Paladin, as guest of honor, sat across from Toria, just to the prince's left, and in this position he was able to observe them both carefully throughout the evening. In fact, from his vantage point, he felt he could see things and perceive things without even quite understanding why.

So preoccupied had he been with the pressures of his royal reception that Paladin had not, until now, noticed the prince's attentions to Toria. This was suddenly more obvious, at least to him. He couldn't even quite identify it. Perhaps it was the prince's body language or his tone of voice or the subtle movement of his hands toward her when he passed the salt or cut her food. Little things each one, but somehow they whispered volumes to Paladin.

And then, of course, there were the prince's eyes. Why hadn't anyone else noticed? They were not merely dedicated to her attention, as an admirer's would be. They were focused, intent upon a quarry like a predator's, peering into forbidden places, but moving so skillfully that they were never discovered or suspected. Frequently those eyes were drawn away for safety. When this occurred their gaze wandered with dissatisfaction and aimlessness until they returned again to the prey.

And yet the true cunning of the prince's lecherous game was that neither he nor his eyes were ever detected, by spectators or victim.

Conversation was commonplace throughout most of the meal. Under the charming social guidance of Peter, the talk dwelt on fascinating topics like the Crimean weather, upcoming soccer championships, and popular vacation spots on the Black and Caspian Seas. Then gradually the discussion drifted, as should have been expected, in Paladin's direction and the niceties of the diplomatic circle.

"And how is your President Phelps?" asked the prince.

"Fine," Paladin faked. "Just fine."

"And does he send any personal regards?" Peter asked expectantly.

"I'm sure he does, Your Majesty," interjected Toria.

"I'm sure he *would*, Your Majesty, but he didn't." Paladin smiled and looked around the table. Toria gave him a look of restrained exasperation—a "Why did you say that?" look. And for the life of him, he didn't know why he had.

"You see," he rambled forward, "I don't really know the president personally."

"However," probed the prince with a glance at Keller, "you are an envoy of his government. You must bear specific greetings to a Royal Head of State." This was a pride issue with the prince. But there was more going on here.

"Certainly, in a sense," said Paladin with slight embarrassment. "Still that isn't to say he sent me here personally. I didn't even vote for the man." He gave a slight laugh.

The prince stopped eating and studied him with an expression of mild ridicule. "Exactly how then can you truly represent President Phelps?"

Paladin looked around. He thought he saw Keller smile. Toria opened her mouth to intervene but Peter silenced her with one intimidating finger and looked back to Paladin. The occupants of the table close at hand were all mildly curious about his answer.

"You misunderstand the workings of a representative government—" Paladin began to explain.

"Misunderstand?" the prince cut him off. "Not surprising." Then he addressed his guests as if Paladin were not there. "Here is a delegate of America, representing a man he didn't even vote for! Democracy! Such a ludicrous concept!"

Paladin's response was instantaneous. "No more ludicrous than the concept of the monarchy."

Suddenly the entire table grew quiet. Paladin felt his guts wrench inside. He cringed and sensed the blood flowing from his head. But most of all he felt the eyes of everyone in the room boring into him.

Why in the world had he said such a thing? He couldn't believe he had heard himself saying the words—words he couldn't seem to stop himself from saying, even as they were coming out of his mouth. The instant mental replay was just as searingly painful, each syllable cutting like a dagger in slow motion.

He was no idiot. He had a certain amount of discretion—a certain amount of good sense. In any normal setting he wouldn't have made such a remark in a million years. There are simply things a man with brains doesn't say—like asking a fat woman if she's pregnant. *No, no, no. Paladin, use your head!*

Worst of all were the frozen expressions on the faces of the guests as Paladin gradually looked up to survey them. All were fairly horrified, with notable exceptions.

Tiomkin's eyes remained fixed on his plate, wisely unengaged.

Colonel Ustinov raised an eyebrow and directed a steady stare at Paladin that was wary and guarded.

Toria blinked her eyes in a mingled display of astonishment and dread.

Worst of all was Keller, whose look of absolute horror was certainly worth provoking, but not at the cost of the vitriol he knew he must ultimately expect from the ambassador.

And then there was the prince. In a split second his entire countenance transformed from mirth to outrage. He had been challenged in his own kingdom, at his own table. What had just happened was never supposed to happen and may never have happened before.

Yet there was that still small voice that seemed immensely pleased, even in the midst of Paladin's discomfort. In fact, the contradiction that the Spirit *should* be pleased added to his frustration.

It occurred to Paladin that now was a good moment for a diversion. "Please pass that caviar, would you?"

The prince was not to be diverted. "What did you say?" he asked with a face of stone.

"The caviar," repeated Paladin. "It is just delicious."

"About the monarchy," clarified the prince.

Toria finally spoke. "Please, Your Highness—"

Keller broke in. "Mr. Smith spoke out of turn."

"I certainly did," Smith readily agreed.

*No you didn't.* The thought came to his head.

"I did," Smith repeated emphatically.

"I don't get that impression," said the prince coldly. "I would like you to explain yourself."

*Go ahead. Explain yourself.*

"Not on your life," said Paladin aloud. He glanced down the

table. Tiomkin was suppressing a well-hidden grin. Ustinov's eyebrow was rising even higher.

"Prince Peter," defended Toria, "Paladin is unaware of the nuances—"

"Your Highness," Keller raised his voice, "Mr. Smith is not authorized to speak on behalf of the United States."

"Then let him speak for himself," said the prince quietly through gritted teeth. "I want to hear his opinion."

"But, Your Highness," said Keller.

"*Silence!*" shouted the prince. The entire room froze. He looked at Paladin without a word. The only sound in the room to Paladin's ears was that annoying still, small voice.

*There. Now what is your opinion?*

Paladin put down his fork and exhaled with irritation. No one at the table quite knew why. If Paladin had never understood how the prophets felt in being "constrained by the Spirit," he certainly sympathized now.[8]

"Very well, Your Highness." Paladin looked him squarely in the eyes. "True, Democracy is a flawed system in that it is only modestly representative. In the case of Arlen Phelps for example, only 52 percent of the electorate voted for him. That is only a little over half. But compare that sample with the people sitting at this table. How many of them voted for you?"

No one spoke. Paladin paused in the dead silence and glanced at Toria who closed her eyes as if to await some unidentifiable impending doom. "At least," Paladin concluded, "that's how I understand it. Do you see?"

Paladin watched the prince, a deliberate picture of outward calm. He held a dessert fork in his right fist, its tines pointed downward against the tablecloth. As the prince looked at him and slowly

---

8. 2 Nephi 4:14—"For I, Nephi, was constrained to speak unto them, according to his word." The Spirit may impress us, on occasion, to do things or say things that we would not necessarily prefer to do or say. Ultimately, being "constrained by the Spirit" is an issue of obedience.

exhaled, the tines began to dig into the linen. Gradually, the tiny fork bent in half until his fist rested on the table. "Yes, I see," he said quietly. "So, you feel a president is superior to a prince?"

In his mind Paladin was pleading with all his heart now. *Please, don't do this to me. Aren't you satisfied?*

*No, not yet,* came the reply. *Be polite. Answer the question.*

Paladin closed his eyes. He opened them again and looked at Peter. "Absolutely not, Your Highness."

He glanced at Keller, who still glared at him with contempt but sighed with small relief. Perhaps he thought that Paladin was going to back off and beg the prince's pardon. If so he was under a gross misconception.

Paladin took a deep breath and continued. "But no man, be he president or prince, has the right to rule without the implied consent of the people. That is the law of civilized nations—and civilized, enlightened leaders."

Paladin looked up and down the table. Every eye was on him now. He slowly stood, picked up his wine glass (of apricot juice), and raised it into the air. "Ladies and gentlemen, a toast to the prince, the parliament, and all who lead the Constitutional Monarchy of Crimea. May they ever stand as they have always stood, as an example of traditional, *yet* representative government to the civilized nations of the world."

Holding his glass aloft, he waited and hoped. Almost in unison his hopes were answered. Everyone at the table stood and raised their glasses to join him in the toast and then, following his lead, joined him in applause, directed toward the prince. Peter sat—stiff, emotionless, surveying the table and the moment. Then gradually a smile broke the ice of his bearded mouth. He nodded in acknowledgment of the toast and the applause and finally an upraised hand gestured toward Paladin. Toast and gesture of diplomacy accepted.

As Paladin took his seat, he casually scanned the table. Tiomkin smiled appreciatively. Keller continued to glare with disapproval.

Toria nodded at the prince, who actually grinned—at which point she stole a congratulatory wink at Paladin himself.

But what gave Paladin particular pause was a penetrating stare from Colonel Ustinov, who sat back and studied him intently. Even as the old soldier's eyebrows leveled, he picked up his wine glass a second time and lifted it in a quiet toast to the evening's "special envoy."

—

Proper, polite, and socially acceptable good-byes had all been expressed for the evening, and Crimea's brightest lights were returning to their cars and limousines. The prince was ignoring most of them, but he took special care to extend his most gracious farewell to Paladin and Toria as he detained them at the massive front doors of the palace. He had completely rebounded to the ultimate of royal amiability.

"You must come again under less confining social circumstances," he beamed. "Receptions are so terribly boring and restrictive. Under more relaxing conditions we might sit at leisure and more comfortably express our minds and thoughts."

Paladin was not convinced. Still his response was polite. "I would love to do so," he said enthusiastically.

Keller, standing behind the prince, was also a picture of pleasantry. "Victoria, dear, would you see that Mr. Smith arrives safely at the embassy? I must discuss a few matters with the prince before I return."

"Certainly, Ian." She turned to the prince. "Your Highness."

Prince Peter bowed slightly, took her hand, kissed it, and then held it for a long moment as he looked at her. Toria gave a light laugh and withdrew her hand awkwardly.

"Until we meet again." The prince nodded and laughed pleasantly. Everyone joined in—for no particular reason—as Paladin and Toria took their leave.

In the instant the huge oak doors closed behind them the smiles and laughter disappeared from the lips of the Prince and the Ambassador.

"That did not go exactly as you planned," spat the prince. He turned and stormed back into the palace proper.

"Perhaps. Perhaps not," agreed Keller, following him. "My objective is to keep him busy as well as to keep him under my thumb. But we *are* learning something of what is on his mind. And we have means of learning more."

Peter stopped, turning on him abruptly and impatiently. "Yes, but there is not a great deal of time."

"That, Your Highness, is in our favor."

—

Outside, Paladin and Toria had walked silently down the long flight of steps leading to the garden drive where the embassy car was now waiting. The lights of the city in the distance sparkled, transforming Rostov into a jewel by night. The smell of the roses carried through the warm evening air to mingle with the chirps of the crickets below them.

As they neared the car and the page who waited there, Paladin finally spoke. "Well, that was quite an evening."

"I should like to have killed you," answered Toria without a pause, cutting in front of him to take her place in the back seat.

But the page did not open the door. Out of the semi-darkness a rich voice spoke in flawless grammatical English, edged with a thick but non-intrusive Russian accent. "That would do little good, Miss Grant. You would soil your dress, and the diplomatic corps would just send another 'envoy.'"

Toria stepped back, startled. "Colonel!"

Paladin took Toria by the shoulders to steady her as he stared into the face of Colonel Ustinov in the dim light. The commander of Crimea's forces stood six feet tall and held himself as Paladin had seen him before, ready to lead.

"I'm sorry if I startled you," the colonel said apologetically. "I've been waiting for a few minutes to see you."

"Paladin," said Toria cordially, "may I present Colonel Dimitri Ustinov, Prince Peter's right hand. Perhaps *he'd* like to kill you—at twenty paces."

"There is no need to introduce us, Miss Grant," said the colonel without a smile. "I believe Mr. Smith and I already somehow know each other. And as for challenging him to a duel—quite the contrary. I've come to congratulate him. You dodged a bullet tonight, Mr. Smith, and very artfully. I must admit I didn't think you could do it."

"Believe me, Colonel," defended Paladin, "I had no intention of offending your prince."

"I believe you. And no apology is necessary. You're an American. You were born innocent, arrogant, and stupid all at the same time."

Paladin smiled and glanced at Toria, who witnessed this candor with wide-eyed amazement. He was grinning with delight by the time he looked back at the colonel. This man was a breath of fresh air. Genuinely truthful, undisguisedly insulting, but totally guileless.

The colonel stood erect, staring Paladin down, man-to-man, waiting for an honest response to an honest challenge. There was something to like in the calloused old soldier. Paladin was instinctively unafraid.

"Colonel, thank you for the most candid, straightforward expression I've heard from anyone since I arrived in Crimea."

"You're welcome," he said without flinching or smiling.

The colonel turned to Toria, who was watching this exchange with dumbfounded awe. "Miss Grant, would you allow me to take a turn in the garden with Mr. Smith, that we may speak privately for a moment? We won't be gone long."

"Certainly," she said. "Are you sure you wouldn't like to shoot him?"

"Sorry," he said with mock regret and opened the limousine door gallantly for her. Once she was safely inside he bowed slightly, shut the door, and began to walk. Paladin quickly kept pace with him.

"May I tell you something?" he finally spoke after several steps. "I love America. But your people are blunt and prideful."

Paladin felt comfortable around the colonel. He could speak his mind. "And the prince *isn't* blunt or prideful?"

"His pride is different," he explained. "It is inbred—the product of generations and built on heredity. American pride is different. It is founded on an assumption that your people are superior to the rest of the world and based on nothing but national identity."

Paladin considered. "That's very observant, Colonel, and you could be right. There's a certain kind of pride that can make a great people. But pride has destroyed far more great kingdoms and empires than it has ever built up. And today, pride has made America a careless nation."

"But a nation is, after all, nothing more than a collection of people," remarked the colonel. "So, the question is, what are your people made of, one by one?"

Paladin had no idea that his simple introduction to this old soldier would be so philosophical. He was actually fascinated. "Well," said Paladin, "I can't answer for anyone but myself. But I wouldn't mind you telling me what *you* see."

"Since you ask," ventured the colonel, "I'll give you an honest answer. I don't believe *you* are consumed with American pride—for the simple reason that you are not the least defensive about it. Miss Grant, who waits patiently in the car, is another notable exception. She is a rare gem in the American Embassy, in stark contrast to Ambassador Keller."

"How *about* Mr. Keller?"

"Ambassador Keller," sighed the Colonel, "is a fool. And he is typical of the arrogance and corruption that will destroy America if America is not more vigilant.

"But your bluntness," the old soldier shifted, "which was so dangerous tonight was not from pride or arrogance or stupidity. I was watching you—the way a commander watches an adversary in battle. You were reluctant to engage the prince, and yet you attacked, and you did so for a reason—which is what I do not understand. I would like to know what your intention was."

For the next few moments the colonel continued to walk through the rose garden at an even pace. He neither spoke nor glanced at Paladin. The wily soldier was giving his intellectual adversary a moment to process his observations to this point. The colonel finally launched a single salvo. "Would you care to meet me to discuss our individual intentions—as well as the goals we each pursue in the service of our countries?"

It was Paladin's turn to be silent and wait. But deep within him there was conversation. The still, small feeling seemed to whisper in sensations no more pronounced than the sound of the crickets or the fragrance of the roses: *Go ahead.*

"I would."

The two of them had just about completed the circular walkway through the small rose garden. The embassy car was waiting just ahead. "I'm reviewing the troops tomorrow from my balcony. I'd be pleased to have you join me. We can talk then. I'll send a car for you in the morning at ten."

"A military vehicle?" asked Paladin.

"A Mercedes," corrected the colonel as he opened the rear door of the limousine. Toria was waiting inside.

"A very interesting friend you have here, Miss Grant. He's no diplomat. But I don't know what to make of him. Good night to you both."

# 9

## The Iron Colonel

**O**N FRIDAY MORNING Paladin arose early to make sure he would have time to email Rachel. Sending her a message directly from the embassy was convenient for everyone concerned. For Paladin certainly.

Unknown to Paladin, it was also easier for Keller to intercept and read. But it also made Keller more curious, more furious, more frustrated, and more confused than ever.

*Dear Rachel,*

*I cannot begin to tell all that has happened since yesterday. The Lord is guiding my footsteps constantly. Your suspicions were correct regarding Victoria Grant. "Hell hath no fury . . ." However, I believe we reconciled those differences by noon. I have not told her the true nature of my mission. Neither she nor Keller must know for now.*

*In the meantime, I was placed on staff with the embassy yesterday morning, and in the evening I was welcomed at a reception and dinner by Prince Peter of Crimea. I had a long conversation with him and spoke as impressed and instructed. That practically got me beheaded. (I'll explain later.) I also met the Prime Minister of Parliament and the Commander of the Army. (The colonel says that Keller is an idiot. I agree with him.)*

*I hope I can finish what I came to do and escape from here soon. Until then, know that I feel I am under the care of the Almighty.*

*I love and miss you.*

*Paladin*

Toria was waiting for Paladin in the dining room when he arrived for breakfast. Keller was absent. The serving maid had just brought her an omelet with a side of toast and a teacup and saucer.

"Good morning, Toria." He sat himself and looked up at the maid. "May I have one of those—with a cup of hot cocoa, please?" The maid nodded and silently disappeared. Paladin looked at Toria's cup. "Is that coffee?"

Toria answered him with an icy stare that indicated the subject was worth dropping.

"Hmm." He looked around. "Where's the ambassador?"

"The ambassador will not be joining us this morning. He is very out of sorts. And it seems to be about more than last night—if last night's performance wasn't enough."

"Please, could we *not* go over that again?"

"Frankly, Paladin, he's getting a little impatient."

"If he's so impatient, why doesn't he demand we talk?" suggested Paladin. "Between you and me, I don't think the ambassador wants to have our little interview."

"Between you and me," whispered Toria, "I don't think you want it either. Neither of you is pressing the issue."

"Well," Paladin paused, "in that case everybody's happy."

"Not everybody." Toria smiled. "*I* still want to find out what you are doing here."

Paladin took a deep, creative breath, looked up at the ceiling, and leaned forward across the table. At that instant the maid arrived with his breakfast. She set it down, and he watched her leave the room. Pausing, he took a sip of the hot chocolate. "Hey, this is pretty good."

"Yeah, I was surprised. I never tried it until this morning. Now," she refocused, "you were about to tell me something."

"Okay," he swallowed. "The State Department is receiving conflicting reports on the political and military intrigue between Russia and Crimea. The president has asked for a first hand analysis of the situation—to assist in reconsidering American involvement. I was assigned under your uncle's responsibility to covertly investigate information received by the embassy for independent verification."

Toria listened politely. She drummed her fingers delicately on the tablecloth and suppressed a yawn. When he was done she spoke. "Paladin, you're much more effective when you tell the truth. Everybody knows that Arlen Phelps doesn't give a hoot for what's happening between Russia and Crimea, and has no intention of getting the United States involved if he did. And you and I know that my uncle doesn't care about anything 'covert' unless it can further his sweet political career 'overtly.' Besides you told the prince you had no personal mission from the president."

"Yeah, well, maybe I was lying."

"Yeah, well, maybe you're lying now."

"Well, maybe you don't know what you're talking about."

"Or maybe I can see right through you!" she raised her voice.

"Oh." Paladin was quiet. "Maybe you're pretty smart."

"You bet I am," Toria said without a beat. "And I tell you one conclusion I've come to. I don't think you're a diplomat at all."

"Well," Paladin smiled in surrender and began eating his omelet, "you're certainly not alone there."

"And yet in twenty-four hours you stroll in here with little more than your charm and are already on a first name basis with the most influential people in the country."

"Most of whom are very nice," he said with his mouth full. "How come everybody here speaks English?"

"Paladin, this isn't California. This is the real world. You know the old joke. What do you call someone who speaks three languages?"

"Trilingual."

"What do you call someone who speaks two languages?"

"Bilingual."

"Then what do you call someone who speaks one language?"

Paladin thought a moment.

"American," said Toria. She continued to drink the rest of her chocolate. Paladin considered briefly. "I speak Spanish."

"Too bad we're in Crimea not Argentina. Ah . . ." She put down her cup. "That reminds me. Are you ready to tell me yet what you and the colonel discussed on your moonlight walk?"

"We visited for five minutes," Paladin said elusively. "Since we weren't able to talk at the reception, the colonel merely wanted to exchange pleasantries."

"Pleasantries! Paladin, we're talking about Dimitri Ustinov. *The Iron Colonel of Rostov.* I've never seen anyone except the prince converse with the man for more than two minutes—ever. And yet he visited with you like an old friend."

"Is he that intimidating?"

Toria put both elbows on the table. "He's feared, and he's honored. He knows where the bodies are buried as well as the nuclear missiles—and the codes to launch them. The people revere him, and his troops worship him. He's probably at once the most respected and the most unapproachable man in the country. They look up to him and they obey him. But no one sits down to chat with him. And now he's invited you over for a morning cup of tea to review the troops together." She paused, and a glimmer caught her pretty eyes as she lowered her voice. "What did he say?"

"He said you're a rare gem in the American Embassy."

She smirked at him. "Right!"

At that moment a Marine appeared at the door of the room. "Ms. Grant, there's a car at the gate driven by a Crimean officer. He says he is here to pick up a personal guest of Colonel Ustinov. He gave no name."

Toria looked at Paladin. "Looks like your ride is here."

"Would you like to come along?"

"I wasn't invited," she drawled. "Perhaps you *should* be a diplomat."

———

Paladin stood on the steps of the embassy staring at the Mercedes that was waiting for him. He turned to the Marine, who had accompanied him to the front door. "Is that a Crimean military vehicle, Sergeant?"

"That, sir, I believe," answered the Marine, "is the Iron Colonel's personal vehicle." He raised his eyebrows. "Have a nice day, sir."

Paladin cleared his throat and descended the steps to the car where the Crimean officer, a captain, waited beside the open rear door, closing it once his passenger was seated. He was certainly being treated as an honored guest.

The short drive through the tree-lined outskirts of town was a pleasant one. Paladin assumed his chauffeur, the captain, did not speak a word of English, because the drive was also quiet.

That did not stop the captain from studying him through the rearview mirror. The scrutiny of his piercing eyes made Paladin feel as if he were trying to figure him out—to unravel some secret about this inexplicable American who had been invited to meet his colonel on such a personal basis.

After a few minutes of this inspection, Paladin smiled with slight embarrassment as he shifted uncomfortably in the backseat.

However, the captain merely nodded and continued to stare without smile or apologies. Finally Paladin decided to end the awkward silence.

"Hello," he said as cheerily as he could.

"*Privyet*," the captain muttered without flinching.

"Do you speak English?" asked Paladin with deliberate pronunciation.

The captain's face remained expressionless. Then he spoke. "A little," he said in a thick accent as he gestured with his finger and his thumb, barely a quarter inch apart.

*A breakthrough,* thought Paladin. *So he does talk.* "Where did you learn?" he asked, still speaking very slowly.

The driver paused and thought, picking out the English words in his head. "Two young Americans teach me. Gave classes. Good teachers."

Paladin grinned. Of course. "Mormon missionaries?"

But the Captain didn't break a smile. "Yes, Mormon missionaries. Good teachers. Good young men."

With the ice broken—sort of—the impulse to share the gospel was suddenly irresistible. "Did they teach you anything about the Mormons?" Paladin ventured.

"Oh, yes," the Captain nodded. "They teach me. They baptize me."

Paladin was momentarily stunned. But then again, why should he be? The LDS Church did have a presence in Crimea. "You'll have to tell me where the chapel is located. I would like to go to church this Sunday."

The captain hesitated. "Oh, I don't go for years."

Paladin sat back in his seat, a bit disappointed. "How come?"

There was a long silence as the captain continued to drive. His eyes no longer searched Paladin's with his icy stare. "You must understand," he spoke haltingly, "a soldier's life is busy. And I am aid to Colonel Ustinov—a great honor. The army and the colonel—these are religion enough for any man."

It was, Paladin supposed, intended as a joke. Yet the captain did not laugh.

Paladin watched him in the rearview mirror and smiled politely.

The captain looked back and sighed deeply. There was another long silence. He was reminiscing to himself. "Yes, I like missionaries. I like Church. Maybe, I go back—someday."

Much like Dimitri Ustinov himself, the captain was as straightforward as he was capable of being, while behind those eyes was hidden a multitude of mystery.

After less than a ten-minute ride, the car stopped before two huge steel gates. The captain blared his horn and the gates opened, admitting them to a small estate on a military compound, after which they came to a stop in front of a modest mansion. The captain stepped around the car to open Paladin's door and motioned for him to follow.

Paladin barely had time to survey the grounds before they stood at the front door, which opened immediately. There, larger than life, stood Colonel Ustinov, who greeted him heartily and invited him in as the captain saluted.

"Mr. Smith, do come in." The colonel routinely returned the salute and closed the door.

The old soldier began to walk with the unspoken expectation for Paladin to keep up. "Your drive was pleasant?"

"Yes, very." Indeed it had been. The outskirts of town were much more beautiful than the city.

They talked about nothing in particular as their footsteps tread upon plush carpet—making comments about works of art on the walls and the historic or military depictions they portrayed. They exchanged observations about volumes of old books, antique furniture, and a suit of armor on the stairway landing.

Finally, as they sat on the balcony, the colonel suggested they have a mid-morning cup of tea. Paladin looked over the railing and saw the beginnings of the parade preparations.

"It's a beautiful thing to watch troops march in unison. I myself have two left feet. I think that's why the US army rejected me."

"Don't be modest," the colonel smiled. "I know a little bit about you. *Four-F.* But you'll still always be an enlisted man."

Paladin lowered his herbal tea momentarily, surprised at the old soldier's personal research.

The colonel continued. "Today's review is really just a preview for my approval. Next Wednesday will be a full military display for Coronation Day, our national holiday—an annual reenactment of the crowning of the king. That day will be in honor of the prince. A Russian military delegation and other foreign representatives will even be present. It will be a day to remember."

Paladin had been listening intently. "Excuse me, Colonel. I know many Crimeans speak English, but your English is much more *American.* Where did you learn it?"

The old soldier sat back reflectively, "I lived in the United States for several years as a young man. I attended New York University and studied military science in Brooklyn." He leaned forward slightly and spoke low. "My hero was George Washington—Battle of Trenton."

Then he sat up and his voice resumed its regular volume. "But when I left America to rejoin the Crimean military, well, I said good-bye to old heroes and old friends. Your Founding Fathers had to make exactly the same decisions. Revolutions and perestroika and the disunion of nations—there is really not that great a difference. To a soldier, all it means is change. But three realities of my life remain constant. Crimea will always be my home, the army will always be my family, and duty will always be my law. The current political climate does nothing to change these."

"Consider the Russian army, for example," Ustinov spoke matter-of-factly. "Most of parliament and the prime minister fear them as invaders. The prince welcomes them as instruments of peace to restore order."

"And what is your response?" asked Paladin.

"Neither, Mr. Smith. To me the Russian presence is military data, nothing more. In reality the army gathering north of Crimea is a relatively small force—not more than 200,000. The sizeable Crimean forces under my command would tip the balance, one way or the other, in any military action. And that decision—to repel them as invaders or to welcome them as friendly neighbors—would not be a choice for me to make."

The colonel took a deep breath and looked out over the parade grounds. "You see, Mr. Smith, politics is not our affair—yours or mine. It is the business of princes, parliaments, and presidents. My father and my father's father before him have lived in the service of the royal family. Loyalty to the king—that is the life and duty of a soldier. And where Prince Peter goes, there go I. My life is pledged to him.

"We agreed to share our motivations and intentions," the colonel summarized. "The service of the prince and the care of 600,000 men and women of the Crimean army—that is my existence. That is my life."

Throughout almost the entire length of Colonel Ustinov's statement, Paladin had remained silent and attentive. The old soldier's objectives could not have been more straightforward. He looked directly at Paladin.

"Now, I have brought you here under no false pretenses to ask you what your intentions are in Crimea. But before you speak, let me make it clear that your integrity and good intentions mean nothing to me because they can be so warped and misguided by the national pride we spoke of. Having said that then, let me ask you directly—why are you here?"

Paladin answered without hesitation, looking the commander in the eye. "I don't know, Colonel. I honestly don't know."

The Colonel put down his tea and studied Paladin long and steadily.

"Or you haven't decided yet."

"Wouldn't the answer be about the same?" Paladin asked.

The old soldier shook his head slightly, then continued, surprising Paladin. "Still, you're not telling me the complete truth. You're holding back something."

Paladin nodded in acknowledgment and moved to the edge of his chair. "I have come to take Victoria Grant back the United States before your country explodes."

The colonel waited, stroked his mustache, and pursed his lips as he considered this disclosure. His eyes finally met Paladin's.

"Since that information is of no possible threat to the prince, there is no reason for me to pass that confidence to him. But understand this. If your presence here does threaten His Highness—you must know where my allegiance lies. And I would not hesitate to kill anyone in his defense. Are we absolutely clear on this matter?"

"Yes, sir."

"Good." The colonel peered into the distance and sighed, satisfied with having made himself understood. He brightened and rose to his feet. "Well, it appears the troops are ready. Let us forget any conversation bordering on politics. At this point it does not appear to be a business that concerns either of us."

Colonel Dimitri Ustinov took a step to the edge of the balcony and gripped the railing. Paladin joined him and sensed the pride of a grandfather beaming as he watched his accomplished progeny. These were the colonel's children—over 100,000 of them on display. The army of Crimea was a power to be reckoned with.

# 10

# THE TRUTH ABOUT MR. SMITH

I**T WAS PAST** one o'clock when Paladin arrived back at the embassy. As he stepped up to the front gate, a young man ran up to him with an envelope, handed it to him, and ran away.

Paladin watched the boy run around the corner and then looked at the envelope addressed to him. Shrugging, he opened it and read it where he stood.

*Mr. Paladin Smith*
*Special American Envoy*
*United States Embassy*

*My Dear Mr. Smith,*
*Please excuse my abruptness last night. Perhaps my appraisal of you was shortsighted. You may yet be able to help us. You don't appear to be in anyone's pocket. You asked me if our own people might not do something. That would depend entirely on the unity of the people. And at present, the people have no voice.*

*But there is someone who does have a voice—a voice that could make a difference—but refuses to make it heard. I should like you to meet Archbishop Basil of the Russian Orthodox Church.*

*At the risk of being too bold, I have taken the liberty of speaking with the archdiocese myself. They will be in contact with you to request an audience.*

*Regards,*
*Yuri Tiomkin*
*Prime Minister*

*P.S. You should be aware—my sources tell me Ambassador Keller is intercepting your emails. Have a care.*

"My emails? But why?" What in the world was going on here? What game was Keller playing? Paladin tried to remember anything he said that Keller might have read and misinterpreted—or properly interpreted—in his personal letters to Rachel. At first, he was angry, then suddenly he laughed, then just as suddenly he was angry again. He had not thought it possible to dislike Keller any more than he already did.

"Wow!" he mused to himself. "I called him an idiot this morning. I'll bet that ticked him off," he smiled. Instantly the smile vanished again. By this time Rachel had doubtless returned his email. "I wonder what she said."

Passing through the gate, Paladin quickly walked up the steps to the embassy and into the office where he'd emailed Rachel earlier. Sitting at the computer, he typed in his password and accessed his account. There it was—a treasured note from Rachel. But somehow as he opened it he felt in his heart that he was reading a letter with the wax seal broken. He read it carefully.

*Dear Paladin,*
*I love you so. I was beginning to worry when I didn't hear*

*from you the first day. But I understand you had a great deal of
pressure on you as well as jet lag. I am amazed at the progress
that you have made in two days. The Lord is truly with you.
But if that is true, remember that the adversary is there too. And
he will do anything to stop you.*

*You are in grave danger. The news talks of it daily. You must
hurry and complete your business and leave Crimea. Please
return to me with your mission accomplished.*

*We pray for you constantly.*

*Love,*

*Rachel*

*Good grief,* thought Paladin. *That must have gotten Keller's attention. It certainly got mine.*

Paladin immediately began to type a new message. It was
going to have to be short. How could he tell her she couldn't write
to him? Anything she said was going to be monitored and would
therefore compromise his efforts.

*Dear Rachel,*

*I'm going to be leaving the embassy today. I won't have
access to a computer for a day or so. Wait until you hear from
me. We'll talk then.*

*I love you.*

*Paladin*

He felt helplessly stupid writing such a message. It was painfully short and agonizingly impersonal. His jaw set firmly and his
teeth clenched as his hands balled into fists. Right now he would
gladly beat Keller in the face, nonstop, for forcing him to do this.
"I wish he were here," he whispered to himself. His eyes leveled at
the screen and lost their focus.

Gradually he loosened his fingers and guided the cursor

115

reluctantly to the end of the toolbar. "SEND." He logged off and stood from the desk. There was nothing but ice in his heart.

"I'll kill Keller another day."

*No, you won't.*

"But do you realize what he's done? What he's doing? He's a poisonous reptile."

*So you've been bitten. Don't waste your time hunting down the snake. You've more critical things to do. Rachel is right. You're in danger—and you're running out of time. Now go!*

Paladin knew exactly what he had to do. The time had come for action. He walked quickly from the office to the lobby of the embassy and into the suite Toria Grant called her work space.

"Paladin," she greeted him, "I had no idea you were back already. How was your tea with the Iron Colonel? Did you learn more state secrets than you gave away?"

"Victoria," he said breathlessly and seriously, "I need to talk to you right away."

"Well, it'll have to wait for a while. I occasionally work for a living, and the Russian delegation is coming in next week—"

"Toria," interrupted Paladin, "do you want me to tell you why I've come to Crimea or not?"

It took Toria approximately a nanosecond to spring from her desk and grab her sweater. No other explanation was necessary for her to be out the office door.

A full minute later she and Paladin had exited the gates of the embassy and were walking to the small public park a half block away. More than once she tried to begin a conversation but both times Paladin made it clear he had no intention of talking until they were off the street and reasonably away from unwelcome listening ears.

The park was a standard plaza with a fountain at the center, but at this time of the day, there weren't many people around. Paladin and Toria sat at the edge of the fountain with the water trickling into the pool behind them. He looked off in the distance considering how to break this revelation. Toria looked on expectantly.

"Okay?" she pressed.

"Toria, what do *you* think I'm doing here?"

She shrugged. "Well, everybody in town has concluded you're not a diplomat. Word has it that the prime minister thinks you're the messiah. The prince thinks you're the Antichrist. *I* think your some kind of government liaison—very hush, hush. What else could explain you? Now, Ian Keller is reserving his opinions. But I believe he's been doing some research."

"That's true," said Paladin bitterly.

"So far he only hints at it. But he says there's a lot more to you than meets the eye. He's actually frightened of you."

"That's rich. Believe me, Toria. I'm nothing to be afraid of."

Toria simply looked at him.

"You know what I really am, Toria? I'm a seminary teacher."

Her eyes narrowed and peered into his. She was waiting—a little more warily now.

"Your uncle sent me to Crimea—to bring you home. That's the long and short of my international mission of intrigue. It's no more complicated than that."

Paladin waited. Slowly the truth dawned on Toria Grant like a gradually crushing weight. As it did, her eyes wandered from his, and the luster left them. She opened her mouth as if to try to inhale some light to fill her again. But suddenly, all was darkness. The only thing to fill her eyes was harsh and empty shock.

She spoke without looking at him. "Oh, Paladin, do you realize the damage you've done?" When she turned to him, her face was full of disillusionment and disbelief. "You come here under false pretenses, posing as a diplomat with a letter from a member of the House, worming your way into international confidences, misrepresenting yourself to a foreign ambassador, and insulting an influential head of state. And for what? To play some game while you satisfy the ego of my idiot congressman of an uncle."

"He was concerned about your safety in this volcano of a country. The whole place is about to erupt. Can't you see that?"

"Philip Chase isn't concerned for anyone but himself and his precious political career. He used you, Paladin. He's made a fool of you and now he's made a fool of me. He sent you here to bring me home because he doesn't want me to embarrass him."

"That doesn't make sense."

"You're the one who said it. My uncle thinks something awful is going to happen here. And when it does, he's afraid I'll be in the middle of it. Congressman Chase doesn't want any bad publicity to stick to him."

"Bad publicity! Toria, if you live through this, it's your connection with Keller that's going to stick to you and everybody else."

"Paladin, stop it! Stop tearing at Ian Keller, because he's certainly been more trustworthy than you."

"Trustworthy? The man is intercepting my email, Toria. I can't even write a note to my wife. And as for getting in the middle of things, you're already there—not just with Keller, who I *don't* trust, but with the prince, who's waiting like a hungry dog to welcome the Russian army into Rostov."

"Paladin, you don't know anything about these things."

"Maybe not, but I know what I feel. And I know people. Prince Peter wants power—and he wants you. Toria, listen to me. Something awful *is* going to happen here and soon. And you *are* in the middle of it. Don't you recognize the way the prince ogles you, favors you, fawns on you? Toria, his attentions are dangerous! He's dangerous! Please, come home while there's still time."

Toria straightened herself and became serious. "Paladin, I'm not a teenager anymore. And I don't need you or my uncle or even the Church to rescue me. Oh, I feel so stupid, because I was actually beginning to believe you. Well, I know something now. This is my home, and this is my job, and this is my life. And I agree.

Something is going to happen in Crimea. But I'm going to stay here to be part of the solution, not the problem."

She buried her head in her hands and then heaved a sigh as she lifted her gaze into the gray sky. "Oh, Paladin, why did you come?"

Paladin felt cold and empty. "I was trying to help."

"You didn't help." Standing, she walked back to the embassy alone.

—

Toria was still upset as she walked through the front entrance of the American Embassy. The ambassador happened to be waiting there and she intentionally brightened when she saw him. He noticed, but ignored the change.

"Victoria, I've been looking for you. Have you seen Mr. Smith?"

At that moment Paladin entered, to the satisfaction of Keller's timing. "Ah, perfect. I need to speak with both of you." He held up a letter. "At the recommendation of the prime minister, Archbishop Basil has requested a luncheon audience with our very own Mr. Smith. The archdiocese has invited us all to join them tomorrow at noon. I have already accepted the invitation."

Toria received the news without emotion. She turned to Paladin. "Oh, hurray. What mischief can you create with the Orthodox Church to make your secret mission complete?" Shaking her head, she disappeared up the spiral stairs.

Keller stood motionless and expressionless until Toria had gone. "Would you care to explain that, Mr. Smith?"

"No." Paladin turned and left the room without a backward glance, slamming the door behind him, leaving Keller alone.

—

On Saturday morning, Keller ate breakfast alone in the dining room. Paladin hadn't come down for breakfast, and Toria had also asked to be excused—she was feeling under the weather.

Keller leaned back in his chair at the head of the table, thoroughly satisfied with life as he read the news from the world's leading papers. The front-page headlines were all about the pending crisis in Crimea. Things were certainly brewing in Eastern Europe. Keller smiled. This was a good morning. He was beginning to feel in control again.

A short time later while he was taking care of some light work in his office, Toria entered, looking slightly ragged and nervous. "Good morning, Ian."

"Victoria, are you feeling any better?"

"Yes, Ian. I'll be fine."

From her appearance Keller was wondering if she had gotten any sleep last night. But abandoning the obvious, he chose another approach. "I'm concerned about your health, Victoria. To be quite honest, I've been concerned about you for the past few days. Ever since that Smith fellow came to Crimea, you haven't been quite yourself."

Toria cleared her throat. "That's actually what I came to see you about," she fumbled reluctantly. "Ambassador Keller, I think you need to know something about Paladin Smith."

# 11

# ARCHBISHOP BASIL II

**T**HE EMBASSY'S LARGEST limousine was scheduled for the afternoon. Keller thought it best that the four of them—Paladin, Victoria, Jeffries, and himself—travel together to the luncheon. "Much more cozy," was his cheerful explanation. And he was as cheerful and talkative as he had been all week.

Jeffries sat attentively during the drive, listening dutifully and laughing appropriately at the ambassador's every witticism. Paladin and Toria, by contrast, were morose and non-responsive. The weather was dull. It looked like rain.

As the driver pulled the car up at the spacious monastery, the passengers disembarked—this time on the east side of the massive Cathedral of the Resurrection, which Paladin had toured earlier. He watched Toria as she took a long look at the huge golden dome, shook her head, and followed the party to the monastery without so much as glancing at him.

The white Cathedral of the Resurrection was separated from the modest monastery by a courtyard and a reception hall, accessible by a dozen small arcades on each side. The embassy representatives were welcomed by a robed priest who was waiting for them by the entry.

"*Privetstvovat!*" he greeted them in Russian.

The three diplomats answered and conversed with him in his native tongue as they passed through the arcades into the court-yard and on into the reception hall.

Paladin couldn't expect everyone in Crimea to accommodate him with fluent English, but today, his inability to communicate made him feel conspicuously out of place.

It was a feeling that was to grow more pronounced. The official home of Crimea's Russian Orthodox hierarchy was a Russian-only atmosphere. Everyone in attendance—the priests, the bishops, and the archbishop himself understood nothing but the mother tongue. Ostensibly, that was one reason that Keller had made certain to bring adequate resources for translation. Interpretation was beneath *him*, but together, Toria and Jeffries were more than up to the task.

Archbishop Basil II was introduced to the embassy party at the entrance to the room. Paladin recognized the elderly man and the long beard. Today he was dressed in a white robe and a white cap and donned a pair of spectacles. He also wore an expression of the deepest gravity and austerity. Paladin couldn't help but wonder if the cleric had ever smiled in his life.

As he studied the archbishop, he recalled the flavorless description supplied by the State Department: *limits his sphere of influence to religious matters, politically moderate, and traditionally loyal to the royal house.* Not only did he appear meek and lackluster, but his unwillingness to involve himself in public affairs hardly qualified him as the potential "voice of the people" that Prime Minister Tiomkin characterized him to be.

The archbishop's greeting initially seemed as cold as his facial features and his biography. Taking Paladin's hand, he welcomed him in thick but soft-spoken Russian. However, the language barrier did not make him reticent. There was quiet power here. He spoke directly to Paladin as if he intended for him to understand every word.

"He says it is a genuine pleasure to greet you to the company of the bishops and priests today," translated Jeffries. "He says he is anxious to hear your thoughts."

"Thank you very much, Your Grace," answered Paladin, while Jeffries transmitted the return message. Paladin's voice fell to a whisper. "Your Grace? Is that the right title, Jeffries? And am I supposed to kiss his hand or anything?"

"Your Grace is fine, Smith," interrupted Keller, behind him in an undertone. "And please *don't* kiss his hand—or do anything else stupid."

He moved away, leaving Paladin a little startled. There was no time to react. The archbishop said something else in Russian. Paladin looked to Jeffries.

"The archbishop suggests we take our places at the table where we can eat and converse more comfortably."

———

Lunch was light and pleasant. But constant translation made conversation tedious. Since Keller directed most of the discussion, it would have been easy for him to eliminate Paladin from the loop and speak exclusively in Russian. But as Paladin watched him, he realized that today was a reestablishment of Keller's power base— for Paladin's benefit. Ambassador Keller's luncheon performance was a demonstration that he had taken charge of his world again.

Though Keller was anxious to humiliate the "special envoy" while he reasserted his own position, he needn't have tried so hard. Paladin was prepared to let Keller have his world. He just wanted to board the plane and retreat from Crimean soil. He didn't belong here. He had failed. All of this was an enormous mistake. How could he have ever supposed that he could bring Victoria Grant back to America—let alone make a difference to international politics?

Toria was right. He was a fool. He'd packed his bags this morning. They were waiting in his room at the embassy. His mission was done. It was time to go home.

The conversation at the table had dwelled on the trivial. But Keller had finally insisted on discussing substantial matters of state, translated into English for Paladin to hear. He wanted his policy understood. All this was slightly frustrating for the archbishop who wished for the "special envoy" to express himself. However, Paladin said little or nothing.

If Paladin had glanced at Toria, he would have seen that even she was pained and shocked at Keller's brashness and Paladin's own surrender. Keller was at the peak of his game. This was his hour—his ascendancy over everything sacred and profane.

The ambassador had for several minutes pontificated on the virtues of professional diplomacy and was in the middle of lecturing the bishops on their ecclesiastical duties in times of political crisis.

"No matter which way the wind blows," he raised his voice as Jeffries translated, "it is the responsibility of the church to bring peace to the people. That is what the Bible teaches. That is what Jesus Christ would have done in the spirit of good will to men."

The mere thought of Ian Keller lecturing these decent men on the principles of scripture or the teachings of Jesus Christ was almost more than Paladin could stand, but he had already committed himself to retire from all argument. This was no longer his battle, if it ever had been.

He gritted his teeth and carelessly picked up his fork to jab at a radish when the utensil slipped from his fingers and fell, clattering on the plate. He made no effort to retrieve it, but simply stared at it, seething. His hands gripped the edge of the table. He was not listening to the idle luncheon conversations. If he had been, he would have realized all talk had ceased. Everyone's eyes were directed at him.

"As I was saying," resumed Keller, but an upraised hand from the archbishop across the table stopped him.

"*Vy ne horosh vyglyadite,*" he said in a concerned voice. "*Vam eta yeda ne po vkusu?*"

Toria, who had been assigned to sit beside Paladin but, to this point, had not uttered a word to him, immediately translated. "The Archbishop notes that you do not look well. Is the food not to your liking?"

Paladin looked up. His eyes were red with emotion. "The food is fine. It is the discussion that is not to my liking."

Toria blinked her eyes and translated for the archbishop, who immediately answered.

"Perhaps you would like to contribute your own thoughts then," repeated Toria.

Paladin turned his head toward Toria but kept his eyes on the archbishop. "No, Your Grace. My opinions are merely those of a lowly United States citizen."

Toria swallowed hard and gave the message to the archbishop, who received it with slight confusion.

"You do not feel inclined to express yourself as a diplomat?" Toria's voice quavered.

Paladin looked directly at her. "No, I don't." She bit her lip and relayed the words to the archbishop, barely above a whisper.

The archbishop, however, did not hesitate. His words were direct and strong. Paladin knew they meant something when Keller cleared his throat and shifted uncomfortably in his chair. Toria got a curious expression on her face and translated in a firmer voice herself. "Then perhaps I would like to hear your opinion as a lowly citizen. Please, I'm sure freedom of speech must be of some value . . . even here."

*All right, Paladin,* he considered, *you may be a fool, but this is a fool's final opportunity to speak the truth.*

The moment he made that resolve he felt the warm power of the Spirit fill him from the top of his head to the soles of his feet. He *was* here for a reason. He smiled faintly at Toria. It didn't matter now what she thought of him. She just had to translate and keep up.

"Very well, Your Grace. My opinion may be considered of little value. I am, after all, only an American citizen and a teacher. Your opinion on the other hand, holds the power to inspire thousands. The weight and worth of your words could influence an entire nation and awaken it from its lethargy in a time of crisis. I am told everywhere that there are critical events occurring in Crimea that may affect the destiny of the nation, and yet—if I am free to speak—" Paladin paused.

"You are," reassured the archbishop,

"With all due respect, Your Grace, you choose to say nothing but seem content to see your vast flock in peaceful bondage rather than independence."

From his seat a few places down, Keller brought his fist resoundingly down upon the table.

Paladin remained calm as he acknowledged the outburst. "Perhaps I've spoken too freely."

Keller didn't wait. "Mr. Smith fails to see the larger picture, Your Grace. The American Embassy isn't blind to the challenges of the church in a changing culture. We represent the most pluralistic society in the world—which qualifies us to offer solutions from our unique experience. Only wisdom can guarantee the continued freedom of religion for this faith."

The pace of the conversation was gaining energy. It was getting a little difficult for Toria to keep up with the translation. But she was still there, and so was Paladin.

"Solutions?" Paladin repeated and looked at the archbishop. "What solutions exactly?"

The archbishop spoke in measured words. "Ambassador Keller," Toria continued to translate, "has offered us the benefit of his experience in preparing for a potential clash between the government and the church." Paladin watched with interest as Toria began to start and stop uncharacteristically through the process. But he also got the impression that it was more than mere linguistic difficulty that was causing her to stumble. The expression on her face implied that Keller's "religious" diplomacy was new to her.

"The ambassador has suggested that a moderate response from the Russian Orthodox leadership to the current political crisis will promote our ultimate survival. He calls it an application of your established separation of church and state—in order to ensure our continuance should the horrors of the Soviet purges ever return."

"Isn't that nice," said Paladin, turning to look at Keller, ". . . and safe."

Keller needed to take control again. "Victoria, you seem to be having a difficult time with the pace of the discussion. Why don't you let Jeffries translate for awhile?"

"But, Ian, I—" she began to protest.

"Victoria!" His voice was firm.

Whatever Keller was up to Paladin didn't have time for it. He couldn't fight a two-front war right now. He was still talking to the archbishop. "'Separation of church and state' is a sound principle of government, Archbishop. Politics should never be allowed to meddle in the faith of a community or a nation. The ambassador knows this."

Jeffries began slowly, but after a false start or two he hit his stride and began to rattle off translated Russian like a professional.

"This standard has made America strong," said Paladin. "But Ambassador Keller has taught you the warped and distorted puzzle pieces of great truth."

As Toria listened to Jeffries translation, her brows knit into worried furrows. She took one glance at Keller, and his icy stare told her to say nothing. Closing her eyes in realization, she finally saw the truth.

Beside her sat Paladin, having just completed his first thought for Jeffries. He nodded and Jeffries proceeded, then stopped, slightly flustered. "I'm sorry, Ambassador. Let me try that again."

*"Etot princip sdelal Ameriku sil'noy."* He repeated. And that is what Paladin heard. Or rather he *heard* those perfectly understandable Russian words—which he understood as perfectly understandable English in his mind. He listened intently, initially amazed at the process—and then, suddenly shocked at the Russian words Jeffries was saying.

"This standard has made America strong," Paladin heard him say. "And I suppose Ambassador Keller has taught you the safest and surest policy in time of political danger—let the government govern, and let men of faith strengthen the souls of men. That the two remain separate, one never meddling in the affairs of the other is the wisest policy for the safety and happiness of a peaceful nation. 'Render therefore unto Caesar the things which are Caesar's; and unto God the things that are God's.' That is the Bible."

Jeffries stopped and smiled. Paladin looked at him, then at Keller. Both looked very pleased with themselves. A quick glance at Toria told him that she was worried. Another glance across the table told him Basil II was waiting for more. The archbishop didn't have long to wait.

Paladin's movement was instantaneous and explosive. His open hands lunged across the width of the table and grabbed Jeffries by the collar in a grip that was suddenly vice-like. With all his strength he dragged the secretary back toward him, scattering food and table settings everywhere until they stared at each other nose to nose.

Jeffries was no longer pleased with himself. Nothing but terror filled his toad-like eyes. Paladin held him there momentarily until the shrieks from the table quieted down. Then through clenched teeth, and in flawless, textbook Russian, Paladin addressed the archbishop in a clear voice.

"Excuse me, Your Grace, but this man is not interpreting my words correctly. As a matter of fact he is distorting their very meaning. May I speak for myself?"

"Apparently so," said Archbishop Basil, raising his eyebrows. "I wasn't aware you spoke Russian."

Paladin released Jeffries and answered in the native tongue of Crimea. "I don't."[9]

---

9. The gift of tongues is a gift of the Spirit that allows inspired individuals to speak in, understand, or interpret unfamiliar languages. It is documented in the New Testament as well as in modern times.

# 12

# PERSONA NON GRATA

**KELLER WAS ON** his feet in an instant. "Archbishop, this is ridiculous! Mr. Smith is overreacting to what is simply a translation error."

The archbishop looked at Paladin, who slowly shook his head. With an expression of conviction Basil looked back to the ambassador. "Sit down, Mr. Keller."

"Archbishop, I strongly protest!"

"'Methinks thou dost protest too much,'" quoted the Archbishop. "That is Shakespeare. Now sit down." Darkness consumed Keller's expression as he silently took his seat.

All eyes moved from the ambassador to Paladin. "Mr. Smith," invited the archbishop, "you were about to speak for yourself, I believe."

Paladin slowly rose to his feet so that every bishop and priest might hear him. "The separation of church and state was a principle designed to ensure that religion remains free from the tyranny of government and that free institutions be protected from the inquisitions of despotic religion. However, where men think to implement complete elimination of religion from public life, they impose a reign of terror more absolute than any dictatorship that has ever ruled—a world without God. For it is only through faith in the Almighty and a commitment to righteousness that a free nation can truly remain free. And only God can strengthen the resolve for truth in the hearts of good men who stand at the head of a great people."

Then he leaned on the table and looked directly into the eyes of the archbishop. "In that sense, there must never be complete separation of church and state—as long as good men live, wise men rule, and saintly men teach. You must take a stand, Archbishop, and be the shepherd Christ intended you to be."

Paladin ceased to speak. All in the room may not have recognized it, but a force filled the hall and touched the hearts of almost every individual at that table. Seconds went by as the power of God sunk deep into the souls of those who listened. There was silence.

One man was not touched by the Spirit that filled the room. Against all restraint Keller stood, the feet of his chair scraping irreverently against the stone tiles of the floor. He was livid. "This man does not represent the diplomatic viewpoints of the United States of America. This delegation will hereby withdraw with a warning to His Grace that this individual is not a member of the American Embassy, and his opinions are no more than the aberrations of a renegade."

Paladin was prepared to defend himself. "I believe I have already admitted that to the archbishop, Ambassador Keller."

"You, Mr. Smith, have nothing more to say in this discussion. You have misrepresented yourself to the American Embassy and to the Crimean government!"

Paladin looked down at Toria, sitting beside him. She stared up apologetically. There were tears in her eyes. "I'm sorry, Paladin," she whispered.

He smiled and shook his head as if to say, "Don't worry about it." Indeed he wasn't. But there was no time to say more.

Keller was continuing as he reached into his pocket and

withdrew a letter. "I am prepared, as a trusted representative of the United States, to serve this notice to Paladin Smith, a fellow citizen, on behalf of Prince Peter of Crimea—revoking any diplomatic or other privileges formerly extended to you."

He slapped the letter on the table in front of him. "Be it known to everyone in my hearing, as of this moment Mr. Paladin Smith bears the status of *persona non grata*—an unacceptable, unwelcome, unwanted person. May you wear it well."

He backed away from the table. "Come, Jeffries . . . Victoria. We'll be taking our leave."

As Jeffries followed like a trained dog, Toria stood. "What about Paladin?"

Keller turned. "Mr. Smith can do whatever he wants, just as he's done since he arrived. But he is no longer my problem." He finished the last thought as he resumed his walk toward the door and the arcades.

Toria glanced at Paladin. He winked and smiled again. "Go on. I'll see you at church."

With an expression of bewilderment, Toria resigned herself to her duty and followed to catch up with the ambassador. As he watched her go, Paladin was struck with an afterthought. "Your Grace, would you excuse me for a moment?"

The archbishop nodded solemnly, and Paladin darted off in the direction of the exit. He overtook the diplomats just outside the arcades, a hundred feet from the limousine.

"Paladin!" said Toria.

"Repentant so soon?" beamed Keller.

Paladin ignored him. "Toria, would you ask the driver to bring me my briefcase? It's in the trunk of the car." Toria glanced at Keller, nodded, and hurried off.

"Ah," said Keller. "I see you've thought of everything."

"No," answered Paladin. "Just a lucky accident. Though I don't really believe in accidents, do you?"

"No, Smith. Accidents are for amateurs. Careful planning always serves me better."

"Like that letter. *Persona non grata.* How long have you had that in your pocket?"

"*Your* letter gave me the idea. But I didn't actually ask the prince for his authorization until this morning—when I realized who you were."

Paladin smiled again. "You have no idea who I am."

"Be that as it may, know that any protection you ever claimed through your diplomatic status has been revoked. You came here to meddle in affairs that do not concern you. You're a small time player, Smith. Things are going on that are much bigger than you are. Stay out."

Paladin gave a single laugh. "I'm already in."

"Then you're going to get hurt," said Keller offhandedly, "and you're going to get others hurt too if you're not careful."

He took a quick glance at Toria beside the car.

Paladin felt released from all pretensions and restraint in the presence of Keller. It felt good. Without hesitation he grabbed the ambassador by the collar and stared him in the face. He didn't say a word. He didn't need to.

"I would advise you to let me go," said Keller coldly.

The voice of the Spirit was just as terse. It felt no need to explain. *Let him go!*

Paladin released the ambassador with a mild sense of remorse. *That isn't how we do things.* He breathed a sigh and smoothed the ambassador's lapels. The driver had just set Paladin's briefcase at his feet.

Keller straightened his own tie as he turned to go. "I remind you that you are no longer under the protection of the United States of America in Crimea. You are on your own."

Paladin considered for only a split second and smiled. "I'm never on my own." Picking up his briefcase, he turned his back on Keller and walked away.

# 13

# REVELATIONS AND CONFESSIONS

**N**ONE OF THE mirth that was part of their ride to the luncheon attended the embassy delegation on their return home. All was absolutely silent. The passengers of the limousine were lost in their own thoughts.

Upon arrival at the embassy, Toria retired to her room without the least explanation.

Keller walked into the main entry, shut the double door behind him and stood alone before the spiral staircase. He surveyed his surroundings. Something was very wrong. This was the world he was to have been in complete control of today. He had made it clear.

"Paladin Smith is no longer my problem," he grumbled to himself. And yet, somehow, Paladin Smith was still here.

Fixing his eyes on the top of the stairs, he climbed them quickly with a determined step. He rounded the corner to Toria's room and knocked. "Yes," she said dully.

"It's Ian," he said, trying to brighten his voice.

There was a pause, and then the door opened. "Please, Ian. I'm very tired."

The ambassador gently nudged his way in. "But I need to talk to you, about your Paladin Smith. It has all been very unfortunate, and I am sorry."

Toria looked at him. "No you're not, Ian. You're not sorry at all."

"Victoria, what happened today . . . Smith brought it upon himself."

"Wrong again, Ian. You escorted him to what you hoped would be the execution of a helpless victim. You goaded him and humiliated him in front of the archbishop knowing you had a broken man. You backed him into a corner ready for the kill, and then something went wrong, didn't it?"

"No!" shouted the ambassador. "Nothing went wrong!" He was almost beside himself with rage.

Toria was calm. "Yes, it did. As wrong as the foreign policy you've been spoon-feeding the archbishop. I was listening, Ian. What have you been serving up as the principles of democracy?"

"The delicacies of diplomacy are intended to ensure survival, my dear."

"Whose survival, Ian?"

"Mine, Victoria—and unless you're very naïve, yours. Don't pretend you haven't learned some of the rules that govern the real world under my tutelage. The law of the jungle is the first rule of diplomacy. If applied properly it passes for international relations in a civilized world. Paladin Smith will find that out for himself soon enough."

"Strike three, Ian. Paladin Smith is playing by a set of rules you don't understand. You already know you can't break him. He won't sell out, and he won't give up."

"Then there are other ways of silencing him. Have you already forgotten what you told me this morning, Victoria? That man is an imposter. He can't beat me at my game. And that *is* reality. Nothing has changed."

She shook her head and turned to the window, speaking to herself as much as to Keller. "Everything has changed."

Keller watched her warily and spoke with deliberate care. "The next few days are going to be critical for Crimea—and for you. You can make a difference here. You may even make history. But I need to know I can count on you—as a professional. Can I?"

She paused for a long minute, not daring to face Keller. It was foolish of her. Even from across the room, the ambassador could sense the fear, like a predator. She mistrusted him now—and he knew it. He waited for her answer, well knowing the form it would take.

"Yes, of course," she finally assured him.

Keller smiled. It was exactly as he expected. Predictably deceptive.

Then Toria tried to be light and carelessly casual. "What *will* become of Paladin?"

"We can't be concerned with Paladin Smith," Keller answered frankly. "He cut himself off from us. Matters now stand as they stood before he came to confuse things."

He was about to leave the room when he stopped and turned to Toria one last time. "Meanwhile, why don't you send the things in his room over to the monastery? He probably has no desire to come here, and I don't think it wise for us to make contact with him again. We have too many serious affairs of state to deal with to waste our time on Mr. Smith. Don't you agree?"

"Yes." Toria turned to him with the brightest smile she could muster. "I suppose you're right."

"Good," said Keller, opening the door. "Then this entire episode regarding Paladin Smith appears to be over."

He walked into the hallway, closing the door behind him.

Rounding the corner Keller slowed as he reached the top of the staircase as if to survey his kingdom. This was his day of conquest. He felt power flowing through his veins. Whatever he could not control he would crush—like Paladin Smith. He would not have to crush Victoria Grant. She would fall back into his orbit. But he could crush her if he needed to. He took a deep breath and walked down the stairs.

Entering his office he looked over the spacious room. This was small-time. In a few days he would be moving up. He wasn't going to miss his position here; neither would he miss pretending to take orders from the State Department or the president.

Keller looked over the mass of papers on his desk. It was nothing more than trivia to him. "Except—" He looked closely. "What's this?"

An envelope from the Russian Embassy marked CONFIDENTIAL lay across his blotter. Keller picked it up, sat down, and leaned back in his chair, propping his feet on his desk. He slit the end of the envelope open with moderate interest, pulled out the document inside, and read:

Dossier report from independent sources on Mr. Paladin Smith of the United States of America and ostensibly attached to the American Embassy.

Classification: Extremely Dangerous.

Keller's feet dropped from his desk, and he sat forward as he read with avid intensity. The report from Russian Intelligence was a full page long, and each notation seized the ambassador's attention with more riveting punctuation than the previous. Suddenly he was aware that he was not breathing and that his mouth was bone dry.

At once, everything fell into place. At once everything made sense—the letter, the cryptic emails, the mysterious statements, the uncanny abilities. And all at once everything was at risk—everything.

Keller slammed down the paper and pressed on his intercom, shouting like a madman as he did so. "Jeffries, Jeffries, Jeffries!" The secretary came bursting into the office. "Close the door!" Keller was on his feet, report in hand, pacing the floor.

"'You have no idea who I am.' That's what he said."

"Who?" asked Jeffries.

"Smith, you idiot! And we didn't." He thrust the paper at Jeffries. "Look at this, from our friends in Moscow."

Jeffries bulging eyes widened in horror as he read. "This can't be."

Keller snatched back the report and began to collect himself. He needed to think. He needed to be calm.

"Mr. Paladin Smith is much more dangerous a threat than we ever imagined. I had wondered if it were safe to keep him here. Now I realize it is not safe to let him go. Get me in touch with the palace right away.

"Oh, and Jeffries," Keller said as an afterthought. "Have someone keep an eye on Victoria Grant. I want to know everywhere she goes and everything she does."

—

That afternoon Paladin and the archbishop sat in Basil's office, surrounded by shelves of dusty volumes. They talked of principles, history, and the freedom of men. Paladin steered away from politics. There wasn't much time for it, and it wasn't his place. Besides, that ground had been laid by more able defenders before him—among them fellow archbishops and patriarchs as well as the prime minister.

Paladin soon found out that the archbishop had begun to soften to the philosophy of his peers for many months. "Where much is given, much is required." And the deepening Crimean crisis had been weighing upon him increasingly for the weeks leading up to the present. But only recently could its influence be compared to anything resembling repentance. And only today had the stirrings of an actual change of heart touched his soul.

Paladin well knew that his eloquence had nothing to do with Basil's invitation to converse in private for the afternoon. What had moved the priests and bishops in the hall that day was the powerful persuasion of the Spirit.

However, the archbishop was still struggling against a personal mind-set. He was of the old school—the school of martyrs. For a good part of his life he had suffered through the Soviet purges. He knew what it was like to endure persecution and be recompensed in progress. The Cathedral of the Resurrection and the Church in Crimea were proof of that.

In spite of having his eyes opened to the machinations of Ian Keller, the archbishop was still not convinced that the influence of the Church should muddy the affairs of state. To a certain degree, his attitude was fatalistic. "If it is the will of God that Crimea fall into the hands of the Russians again, the Church will continue to survive. The worship of God will still rule in the hearts of good men."

Paladin's argument was simple. "I don't pretend to lecture Your Grace on matters of religion. But God's children can only come to Christ through the exercise of their agency. This is a matter of conscience. And the true choice of the conscience can only be accomplished by a free people who surrender their own desires voluntarily to the will of God."

The archbishop was thoughtful. "I can see why the prime minister wanted me to meet you. Your rationale, like his, is very logical and very passionate. But his argument is against Alexander Trotsky and Prince Pyotr—and these are purely political issues."

"Your Grace, I speak against no man. And neither need you, for this is not a political issue. The freedom of man is, at heart, a moral issue."

The archbishop looked up at him slowly. "If," continued Paladin, "the rumors concerning Peter and his alliance with Alexander Trotsky are true—if he does intend to betray Crimea into the hands of Russia for his sole political gain—then I beg you to consider these words: *A prince, whose character is thus marked by every act which may define a tyrant, is unfit to be the ruler of a free people.*"

The archbishop said nothing for a minute as he considered. "That is a very ponderous proposition, Mr. Smith. It is also treasonous."

"I realize that. So did those who said it," admitted Paladin. "It is statement from the Declaration of Independence."

The archbishop cleared his voice and shifted in his chair. He needed to change the subject. He sighed deeply as he temporarily shelved these topics in his mental library.

The old man glanced thoughtfully at Paladin. "You impress me as a good Catholic boy."

"I take that as a compliment, Your Grace, but I'm a good Mormon boy."

The archbishop said nothing as he was momentarily taken back.

Paladin moved forward in the silence. "Our missionaries aren't allowed in your country any longer—I believe at your personal insistence."

"You must understand, my friend," explained the old man apologetically, "the Mormons were troublesome."

Paladin nodded his head and peered into Basil's eyes. "So were the apostles."

Paladin wasn't sure, but he thought he saw the hint of a smile steal across the archbishop's thickly bearded face and disappear.

The conversation gradually disintegrated into small talk. The archbishop actually seemed to be enjoying himself. The two parried questions and answers about philosophy and religion. Nothing very deep and nothing very important. It was the old man's way of winding down after a very stressful day. Finally he asked a simple question.

"Where did you learn Russian?"

Paladin opened the archbishop's Cyrillic scriptures to 1 Corinthians 14 and pointed to verses 12 and 13.

*Even so ye, forasmuch as ye are zealous of spiritual gifts, seek that ye may excel to the edifying of the church.*

*Wherefore let him that speaketh in an unknown tongue pray that he may interpret.*

The old man glanced at the scripture and then at Paladin.

Suddenly the archbishop was on his feet. Paladin realized not only that the interview was over, but also that Basil had made a decision—and he had made it a few minutes ago. Their "chat" had indeed been mere relaxation, in preparation for an evening of hard work.

"Mr. Smith, it has been a pleasure. But I must take my leave of you. I need to counsel with the bishops and meet with my clerks immediately. I only have a few short hours to make up the time I have wasted over the last fifteen years. Because you're right. We *are* on the eve of destruction. And if I do not act now, there will be no other time to act."

The archbishop began to walk to the door that led to a large adjoining chapel.

Paladin was overwhelmed by the power of the man's decisiveness.

"Then I'll bid my farewells this evening." He stood and followed him into the chapel. "I'd like to go to church in the morning if you can help me find one. In the meantime, I need to consider what *I'm* going to do next. May I pray in one of your side chapels?"

Basil was slightly curious. "Is that appropriate for a Mormon?"

"No, not really. But if God doesn't find out I've been here, it'll probably be okay." Paladin smiled.

The archbishop didn't. "That is why I call the Mormons troublesome."

Paladin grinned. "Father, we needn't oppose each other when there is so much in this world we already oppose together."

The archbishop stared into Paladin's face for what must have been at least thirty seconds. Then he reached up with his left hand, placed it on Paladin's head, and gently pressed him to a kneeling position before him. Bowing at the feet of Basil II, Paladin looked up with uncertainty as the archbishop made the sign of the cross.

"Bless you, my son," the old man whispered as a tear rolled down his cheek.

He removed the weight of his left hand from Paladin's head and extended his right hand toward him. Paladin took his hand, unsure of what to do next. The archbishop smiled. "Please don't kiss it—or do anything else stupid."

Pulling the younger man to his feet, the old cleric took Paladin's hand lovingly with both of his. Then releasing his grasp, he turned and walked slowly from the chapel. Paladin was left alone.

—

Early Sunday morning it was announced to the entire nation of Crimea that Archbishop Basil II would deliver a pastoral address to the church.

The bishops and priests in every diocese and parish spread the word to every member. News was carried over the airwaves and in every morning newspaper. The very unexpected nature of the sermon was guaranteed to carry on the breeze. Basil had not made such a public pronouncement to the nation and those abroad for over five years.

His address, doubtless a statement related to critical current events, was sure to be important. But gauging from the archbishop's relative silence on matters of public policy, no one had any idea what his statement would be. That alone made the nation, not merely the church, very curious.

Early in the afternoon television camera crews arrived at the Cathedral of the Resurrection where Archbishop Basil would give his address. Though he was over eighty years old and had been preparing throughout the night, he appeared animated and energetic as he entered the chapel. And though he had not appeared before his multi-million-member flock for an occasion such as this in several years, it was apparent that he was no stranger to expressing himself in public.

No, he had passed this way before.

Additionally, the past twenty-four hours had wrought a change in him. He was a man with a bishopric, a divine calling, who knew what he must do. The church was hungry for direction. Basil II had finally come to feed them.

At precisely 2:00 p.m. the radios and televisions of Crimea tuned in to listen to the spiritual leader of the nation speak to them. Newspaper and Internet resources were also waiting by their keyboards as the archbishop stood up to speak.

As near as could be translated, the historic message began, "When in the course of human events . . ."

# 14

## WORDS THAT MOVE NATIONS

PALADIN, HOWEVER, NEVER heard the sermon. He had spent a long night in prayer and study. He was assigned a room at the monastery and a companion/guide from the Orthodox administration.

So it was that Brother Cyril, a younger, brown-frocked monk, happily attended to Paladin's every need in an environment that was so foreign to him.

Cyril was a contrast to the older priests in that he spoke a halting, but passable English, which Paladin found to be an advantage throughout the evening as his Russian gradually slipped away. Still the bond of communication and friendship was quickly established.

Cyril had been in the reception hall that afternoon. But even those who were not were well aware that a momentous event had occurred, with bishops coming and going and the archbishop sequestered with them for the duration of the night in prayer and council. Something significant was going on. The entire monastery knew of it.

That Sunday morning, Paladin arose early to venture an email to Rachel, come what may. Brother Cyril directed him to the administration offices where he sat down and hurried off a note to his wife.

*Dear Rachel,*

*The intrigue here is thicker than the plot of a Tom Clancy novel. I spent the last evening at the Russian Orthodox Monastery. Very nice people. Had a long meeting with the archbishop. Did everything but leave him a Book of Mormon. Maybe next time.*

*This place is going to go off like a firecracker any time now. (I guess you know that.) I'm still not sure how this is going to turn out. But I know the Lord is with me, and I know I am here for a reason. I will be home to you as soon as I can.*

*Know that I love you.*

*Paladin*

He punched SEND and stared at the screen. Then he looked over at his briefcase, which he'd packed that morning with everything practical he had brought to Crimea. (The rest he had been impressed to leave behind.)

Leaning over the desk Paladin picked up an index card and, scrawling a quick note on it, stuffed it into his pocket. Then he stood up. "Okay, Brother Cyril," he said enthusiastically, "let's go to church."

"I do not think that is something I should do," stammered Cyril reluctantly in broken English.

Paladin picked up his briefcase. "Now, Brother," he reasoned, "I won't be coming back here. I'll try to find some family who will take me under their wing at the church. But I've got to *find* the church, and you are my sole guide. I need you to take me there."

Cyril nodded. "All right. I will take you."

"Besides, you might like it." Paladin smiled.

Brother Cyril became very serious. "I *will not* like it!"

"I know, I know," Paladin reassured him. "I was just kidding."

Brother Cyril led the way from the offices to the exit. "The archbishop says the Mormons are troublesome."

"Yes, I know that too," agreed Paladin as he followed him.

———

Paladin and Cyril had just crossed from the arcades to the parking area where a car was waiting.

Something was making Paladin uncomfortable.

Some foreboding came on him instantly and gave him a feeling of dread. But it wasn't distinctive enough to be a warning, or a prompting to action—merely a premonition.

He had an instinctive desire to get into the monastery car as quickly as possible. But before his hand touched the door handle, he felt a powerful grip upon his shoulder.

"Mr. Paladin Smith."

He turned to see an officer of the Crimean Army flanked by two other soldiers, both with their sidearms drawn and pointed at him. Other soldiers stood behind them. The officer continued.

"You are under arrest for sedition against the state of Crimea. You will come with me, please."

Paladin looked at Brother Cyril, whose brows were knit in confusion. "I will tell the archbishop."

"No," said Paladin. "Go to church," he whispered in Cyril's ear. "Tell the girl." He took the index card from his pocket and stuffed it into the monk's hand. "Give her this."

Brother Cyril brightened. "Yes. Yes. I'll do that."

With that Paladin was unceremoniously pulled away and led several paces to a military vehicle that had just pulled up. The door to the backseat opened, and Paladin was shoved inside by the officer, who then got in.

But they were not alone.

Ian Keller waited there, smoking a cigarette. "I apologize if my smoking bothers you," he said without looking at Paladin.

"That's all right," said Paladin. "It's your car."

Keller exhaled. "I told you that you were in over your head. I told you that you were playing with fire. I told you not to meddle in things that were bigger than you are."

"You told me not to mess up your plans," clarified Paladin.

Without warning Keller slapped him in the face. He eyed his prisoner with contempt. "I also told you to get out before you hurt yourself—and others. Not that I care the least about you."

"Don't fool yourself, Keller. You don't care the least about Toria either."

"Maybe not. But she does fit neatly into the plan. And you're not going to mess up anything." Keller opened the door and set one foot on the pavement. "You're about to disappear from Crimea, Mr. Smith."

—

The ambassador stepped out of the backseat, nodded to the driver, and then watched as the car sped away. He threw his cigarette deliberately to the ground and crushed it out. Jeffries stood waiting for him.

"Jeffries, I want you to expunge any evidence that Mr. Paladin Smith was ever attached to or even a visitor to the American Embassy. I want him to vanish from existence as completely as anyone with the label *persona non grata* could hope to be. Do you understand?"

—

The Rostov Branch of the Church of Jesus Christ of Latter-day Saints met on the corner of Yalta and Dubovka Streets in downtown Rostov. It was a modest meetinghouse, but the Church in Salt Lake City had justified its construction in recognition of the rapid growth of the branch and the strength of the members.

President Gorky was a caring, insightful, and spiritual

man—and a great shepherd over his growing congregation. He was, however, nearsighted, and never seemed to have his spectacles with him—which was why it was ideal that his first counselor, Brother Perov, was blessed with 20/20 vision.

In President Gorky's experience, the best gauge of activity of the Rostov Branch was the panoramic view of sacrament attendance from the stand each week. So it was, during those few precious moments prior to the meeting while the prelude music was playing, that the branch leadership took its most important statistical input for executive decisions.

It was about 9:55 a.m. and most of the branch was already seated.

Gorky and Perov sat next to each other on the stand. "How do we look, Brother Perov?" asked the branch president, who had forgotten his glasses.

"Everybody's here," said Perov.

"Any investigators or visitors?" asked the President.

"One," whispered the Counselor. "I don't think I've seen her before. She just walked in. Young woman—American—very pretty."

"Did she come with anyone?"

"No. As a matter of fact, she seems to be looking for someone."

"Well, is this the Church of Jesus Christ or not?" asked Gorky in frustration. "Is anyone going to welcome her?"

"It's all right. Sister Petrokovitz is talking to her now. They're sitting together."

"Good." The president calmed down. "I'm going to begin the meeting." He started to stand.

Suddenly Perov caught his arm. "Not quite yet. There's someone else at the back doors."

"Somebody new?"

"Absolutely."

"Another investigator perhaps?" asked Gorky.

"I doubt it," answered his counselor blankly. "He's wearing a monk's frock, and he just made the sign of the cross."

—

It goes without saying that no amount of fellowshipping could have made Brother Cyril comfortable in the Mormon congregation. President Gorky, a convert from the Orthodox Church himself, was more than sensitive to that reality. Delaying the start of the sacrament meeting, he stepped from the stand to personally greet the monk and ask him what in the world he could do for him.

Cyril was grateful. In President Gorky he had found a kindred spirit in an alien religious world.

"I'm looking for an American girl. She has a friend who is in trouble."

At that moment, Brother Perov arrived from the president's office with his glasses.

"Thank you, Anton. That ought to make things easier." President Gorky placed the spectacles on his head and blinked a time or two, surveying the congregation. All at once he saw her and pointed. "Is that the one by any chance?" Toria had just turned to see the commotion.

"Yes!" said Cyril with elation. "That is her!" Toria recognized him instantly from the luncheon the day before and jumped to her feet.

"Miss," Cyril said in a voice that carried through the chapel, "your friend, Paladin Smith, has been arrested."

"What?" she said as she hurried to him. "On what charge?"

"Sedition or treason. I don't know," Cyril tried to explain. "He asked me to come here to tell you and to bring you this message."

Toria took the 3 x 5 card from the monk and read it. *Prepare to leave. Travel light. Have faith.*

Throughout this exchange President Gorky had been looking

between them, aware that something important was going on, but unable to make anything of it. She looked at him. "Oh, excuse me," she said urgently. "I'm sorry to have been so disruptive, but I've really got to go."

"I can see that," observed the president, "but before you leave—who are you?"

"My name is Victoria Grant."

Gorky raised his eyebrows. "Ah, so you're Victoria Grant. We've wanted to meet you. You're on our membership records. But there was never a way for us to breach the protective walls of the American Embassy to make contact with you."

"You knew I was here?" responded Toria, somewhat stunned. Even Brother Cyril was thoughtfully impressed.

President Gorky merely nodded and patted her hand. "It's good to finally meet you."

"I apologize that I've never come before and that I can't stay now."

"No, no," said President Gorky. "I understand that you have urgent business. But will you come back?"

Toria paused for a moment, and then spoke. "I already have."

—

When Toria returned to the embassy, it was nearly noon. She found Ian Keller in his favorite lounging chair reading the morning paper and smoking a pipe—the picture of relaxation. Before she had a chance to open her mouth, he spoke without looking up from the news.

"And how did you enjoy church this morning? I thought the Mormon services were longer than this." He looked at his watch. "I didn't expect you back so soon."

Toria stood, perplexed. "Are you spying on me, Ian?"

"My dear Victoria," Keller lowered his paper, "it's my job to know what my staff is up to—your interests, your whereabouts. Tell me, was the sermon enlightening?"

"Yes, it was." Toria pulled together her reason. "I learned that Paladin Smith was arrested this morning."

Ian put down his paper and removed his pipe. "Well, this is deep doctrine for the Latter-day Saints. I thought we agreed that Smith was no longer our concern."

"If we agreed to such a thing, then why did *you* have him arrested?"

"Me? Why on earth—"

"Stop pretending, Ian. This has your fingerprints all over it." Toria began to slowly circle the ambassador. "You're starting to worry me. I've never seen you behave with such paranoia. What has Paladin Smith found out?"

Flinging the newspaper aside, Keller was instantly on his feet. "Nothing!" He calmed himself. "Smith doesn't matter anymore. If you must know, I did have him arrested under the authority of the prince. And by that same authority I threw him aboard a nonstop airplane to New York—deported, expelled from Crimea."

Toria was speechless. "You can't."

"I can, and I did. And the prince was only too pleased to comply. Smith has no diplomatic immunity here. *Persona non grata.* No, my dear, that man will not get in my way again."

Toria turned, crestfallen, and walked numbly to the door. As she reached it she took the knob and clung to it to steady herself. "Ian," her voice was emotionless, hardly above a whisper. "Did he say anything before he left?"

Keller's eyes were cold, and his smile like ice. "No." He picked up a page of his newspaper and sat down again, satisfied with his cruelty.

Toria opened the door and froze there momentarily. "I understand the archbishop is giving a pastoral address to the nation at two o'clock today."

Keller resumed his reading. "Nothing that old man can say is going to hurt me either."

Toria left the room. He paid no attention to her.

—

Just as Paladin never heard the address, neither did Keller. At 2:00 p.m. Keller was still lounging in his favorite easy chair reading the fantasy of global events as created by the media outlets of the world. A deep and complex fiction had consumed his mind—and he took comfort in two false realities: that the influence of Paladin Smith had been neutralized and that the ramblings of some *old man* could never affect his personal ambitions. Both were gross misconceptions.

While Paladin and Ian Keller were not listening to the sermon, most of the rest of the nation was. When Archbishop Basil II finished delivering his pastoral address at 2:34 p.m., the people of Crimea were stunned. The archbishop had forcefully reminded them of the key international current event of their time—the reality that Russian troops would soon be visiting their country.

"Prince Pyotr has advised us that 'the coming army promises stability in times of economic and political crisis. It may even mean the beginning of a new relationship with the Russian people that could create a stronger Crimea.' And of course, we, the people, trust our beloved prince. But is the well-being of Crimea really to be brought as a dispensation in the open hands of an invading army and thrust upon us by force? The gifts of a strong nation and a free people are offerings we can only bestow upon ourselves, as we did when we separated from the Soviets years ago. And the blessing of liberty can only be rewarded by God and His Christ upon a people who have the wisdom to decide for themselves through the institutions they have established for the free exercise of their agency."

*Agency!* Now there was a word the Crimeans had not heard used in that context before.

The archbishop went on. "This is a fundamental truth revealed from the world's foundations—a truth affirmed in the sacrifice of the blood of Christ for the dignity of the race—that all God's creatures were henceforth endowed with inalienable rights; that among those rights are life, liberty, and the pursuit of happiness. That to secure these rights, governments, by the grace of God, are instituted among men, deriving their just powers from the consent of the governed—not from popes, not from princes, and certainly not from invading armies promising to bestow those rights upon them in the guise of dissolving the institutions they already possess and taking the populace unwillingly captive."

No one had ever heard the archbishop speak with such power before. In fact, no one had ever heard the archbishop use such terms and phrases before. Much of the address seemed familiar to some students of political science, but they couldn't quite put their finger on its source. Not that it mattered. The heart of the sermon came from the heart of the archbishop.

When he completed his lecture on history, politics, religious responsibility, and principles of liberty, he concluded with these words:

"My children of the Church, let us commit, let us resolve, let us act—for time has run out. Let us move forward with a firm reliance on the protection of God and His Son Jesus Christ our Savior, mutually pledging to each other our lives, our fortunes, and our sacred honor. Amen."

Everyone agreed that it was a heck of an ending. The entire pastoral was electrifying. The archbishop had said things no one else would dare say, things many had wanted to say, and things that many, many others had paused to consider the value of saying.

Newscasters featured it in their broadcasts. Papers wrote about it in their columns. People spoke about it in bars, in taxis, and in lines at corner stores. And families discussed it around the dinner table. Something was happening in Crimea—something Ian Keller could never understand.

# 15

## SECRETS IN THE DARK

**P**ALADIN AWOKE OUT of a restless sleep. Only the barest light allowed him to make out the outlines of the four walls that surrounded him. He shivered as he sat up and tried to orient both his mind and his eyes to his quarters.

Where was he? He'd been so many places the past week—all of them foreign to him. His current lodgings gave him no reference points. Only cold and darkness.

Paladin tapped his feet on the stone floor and smelled the musty odor of damp soil. Dirt, rocks, underground.

He pulled the grubby blanket that had been thrown at him the night before over his shoulders and began to remember. That was it. He was under arrest. He was in prison. And not just any prison either. He was a guest of His Highness Prince Peter of Crimea in the dungeons of the Royal Palace.

"Not everyone gets treated to an honor like this." He coughed as his eyes adjusted to the light.

Groping to his right Paladin found the scarf that he'd been

using as a pillow and wrapped it around his neck. He sat on a wooden cot with leather straps stretched across the frame. Besides his thin wool blanket, there was no other bedding. The walls were blank—a patchwork design of the stone masons who built the foundation of the castle hundreds of years before. The only break was the iron grate that functioned as the door of the cell and allowed a view into the almost pitch-black corridor beyond.

The dimensions of the stone room were about eight feet in all directions.

"It's really not that bad," Paladin mumbled to himself as he looked around. He shivered, and adjusted the scarf again. "I had a dorm room in college that wasn't that much bigger."

Suddenly in the darkness, with all senses operating fully, Paladin heard a sound. A doorway was opening a long way off. Footsteps were approaching from a distance.

He glanced at his watch, its display giving the only light in the cell. It was 9:15 a.m.

Paladin closed his eyes and repeated the same silent prayer he'd uttered the night before. "Lord, make me equal to this task."

He waited until gradually he saw the light of a lantern begin to illuminate the corridor. The footsteps were growing closer. However, there was no conversation to accompany them.

Paladin stood at the cell's grated door to see two individuals walking toward him. Finally about five feet from the door they stopped, shining the light of a flashlight directly into his face.

"Are our accommodations to your liking?" It was the voice of Ian Keller.

"Exactly what I'd expect, Keller," Paladin answered, "though I could do with some breakfast. I haven't had anything to eat for about a day."

"Of course. Jeffries, why don't you ask the maid to get Mr. Smith a nice tall glass of cherry juice?" Keller flashed his light into the face of Jeffries, who looked stupidly uncertain for a moment. Keller laughed at the expense of his secretary and then turned to taunt the prisoner again. "But, this is visiting hours, not feeding time."

"A man certainly learns who his friends are in a situation like this." Paladin smiled. "You know you're the only person who's come to see me since I was thrown in jail."

"It is the least I could do." Keller sat down on a stool in the corridor and continued. "Did you know that the very cell you're standing in was constructed with the original castle in 1790? That structure was burned to the ground in the mid 1800s, and the palace above us was rebuilt on the existing foundation. No prisoner has ever escaped from the dungeons of the Royal Castle."

"Thank you for that encyclopedic guide, Keller," said Paladin. "You should give palace tours for a living."

Keller looked around the edge of the door and examined the iron bars of the grate. "With you safely behind these stone walls, I can resume what I do for a living—without interference."

"And exactly what is that, Keller?" Paladin stared through the grate. "Just who *do* you work for?"

Keller smiled and shrugged. "I work for myself, Smith. I freelance. And although I'm technically employed by the Department of State, I've got a small verbal contract on the side right now with Alexander Trotsky and the prince of Crimea. You see it's my job to use my personal talents and influence—and America's prestige—to keep all the chess pieces here in line."

Paladin smiled. "But, if I'm not mistaken, the bishop on the chessboard is now out of place."

"It's too late for that to make a difference, Smith."

"You don't say that with confidence."

Keller's face darkened. "You'll see. It has also been my duty to see that the United States does not become involved—and that tomorrow evening's transfer of power occurs without incident."

"So the Russians are coming—and you're opening the gates."

"Only heralding the way of the new order," boasted Keller. "The current US administration is willing to believe anything I tell them and prefers non-involvement anyway. But the American public can be so irritatingly sympathetic to the underdog. A poor Eastern European nation engulfed into the massive Russian Federation by military invasion. It all sounds so ugly."

"Much uglier than the sham of a peaceful transfer of authority you intend to sell to the world public."

"You know better than most," said Keller smugly. "You're an advertising man. If packaged correctly, they'll buy it." Keller stood. "Today the Russian army is poising itself at the border. Tomorrow the Crimean Forces will be in place to support them in the name of the prince. And by Wednesday morning parliament will be dissolved by the will of the people—and Prince Peter will be coronated on the real throne of this kingdom."

"Which means Alexander Trotsky will be the new president of Crimea," clarified Paladin. "I don't suppose even Peter the Mediocre is aware of that."

"He doesn't need to know the details. The prince will have served his purpose. And like me he will have been amply paid."

"And where will you be?"

"In a Swiss chalet—enjoying a Russian-supplied bank account and the fruits of my labors."

Suddenly, a commanding voice spoke from behind him in the corridor. "Ambassador Keller," Keller and Jeffries turned with a start. Their flashlights illuminated the face of Colonel Ustinov. "What are you doing here?" he demanded.

"Visiting with the American prisoner. It is my right."

Ustinov glared at him. "It was my understanding that only the prince, the guards, and myself were to be aware of this prisoner."

"I was one of the exceptions," Keller challenged.

"Get out! And take your toad with you. Guard!" he barked in Russian to the palace soldier who had accompanied him. "Please escort the ambassador and his secretary back to the palace. And guard . . ."

"Yes, Colonel?"

"I'm told this prisoner hasn't been fed since yesterday. See that he is brought breakfast immediately."

Ustinov waited until the guard and his charges had disappeared down the corridor before he turned to Paladin. His face by the light of his flashlight was stern and cold. "I told you I could not tolerate any treachery against the prince."

"Treachery? You realize Keller and Trotsky are using the prince."

The colonel was not to be sidetracked. "It is you, not they, who is in prison. You, not they, who has been accused of sedition."

Paladin spoke plainly. "I have committed no crime against His Majesty."

"You spoke at length with the archbishop."

"Isn't that allowed in a free republic?"

"No more than shouting 'fire' in a crowded theater," said the colonel gravely. "Do you realize what has happened in the past twenty-four hours?"

Paladin was bewildered.

The colonel spoke in measured sentences. "Yesterday the archbishop spoke to the nation. Last night the nation slept on it. This morning the nation awoke. It began with protesters in the streets and continued with transit strikes, communication strikes, labor strikes, and rioting before parliament and outside the palace. The people know that a Russian force gathers on the borders. They have known of it for some time. But suddenly they are fired to resistance. They refuse to submit peacefully to Alexander Trotsky—or to Prince Peter. I have had to call up 100,000 troops from the interior to maintain order. *You alone* have created this uproar against His Majesty. And that makes us enemies—my friend."

"Have you come to kill me?"

The old soldier appeared careworn in the lamplight. He looked at Paladin and shook his head. "I will leave that decision to the occupying army."

"So you stand with Alexander Trotsky and the Russian forces."

The colonel raised his voice. "I stand with the royal house of Vasili-yevich. I am the prince's servant." He paused a long moment. "Last week we spoke of your pending decision. I wish you had not made it."

"Colonel Ustinov, you must know my decision was made out of loyalty to the people of Crimea and their government."

"And you must know my decision is made out of loyalty to their prince."

The colonel nodded, turned, and walked down the corridor, leaving Paladin in darkness.

—

Toria's alarm rang at 3:00 a.m. She rolled over in bed and quickly shut it off. The buzzer was set hardly above a whisper, but to her it seemed as if the sound would wake the whole neighborhood. She especially dreaded the thought of disturbing the slumber of Keller or Jeffries.

She lay in the darkness and stared at the clock. In reality, she needn't have set the alarm at all. She hadn't been able to sleep a wink since she had pretended to retire several hours ago.

Toria threw back the covers and climbed out of bed, making her way by the dim outside light to the small desk at the window. She turned on the tiny lamp beside the telephone and studied the number she'd looked up and left there earlier. Glancing at the clock on her bed stand, she considered the time difference again.

"Yes," she thought, "it's about ten hours ago there. That would make it about 7:00 p.m., Monday night." She nervously dialed the number and waited.

"Hello?" said a woman's voice on the other end.

"Hello," said Toria quietly, "is Paladin Smith there?"

There was silence. "No, Paladin's out of the country." The woman made the statement with a note of sadness. "I'm not sure when he'll be back."

"But he's supposed to be back now," said Toria in a higher pitch. "They sent him back—expelled him. He's got to be there."

The response was instantaneous. "Who is this? What's happened?"

"I'm with the embassy," answered Toria. "I'm a friend of his. I don't exactly know what happened. He was arrested and—"

"Are you Victoria Grant?"

Toria's breathing stopped. Someone knew who she was. Her heart leaped to her throat. "Yes, and I'm so scared. Is . . . is this Rachel?"

"Yes, Victoria, this is Rachel. Now, tell me, what's going on? Where's Paladin?"

"I don't know." Toria struggled through her tears. "Paladin arrived on some secret mission (though he really came to take me back to America), but then Keller, who's plotting something with the prince, attached him to the embassy until Paladin met and talked with the archbishop, who gave a pastoral address that got everyone rioting—and now the whole country is upset, the Russians are invading, and the government's about to collapse—"

"Victoria, Victoria, Victoria!" soothed Rachel rather forcefully. "Slow down. What happened to Paladin?"

"Paladin—" Toria took hold of the thought and calmed herself. "The prince revoked his protective status and declared him *persona non grata*. That's pretty much 'pariah' among foreign personnel. An unwelcome person. It's our lowest life form. Without any international protection, he was arrested and then deported from the country on Sunday."

There was another long pause over the line. Rachel spoke into the phone again. "But, Victoria, he's not here. If he'd been on his way, he'd have let me know. How do you know he was sent home?"

"Ian Keller told me."

"Keller!" blurted Rachel. "Victoria, I know a little bit about him. And you can't trust him."

"I know," Toria's quavering voice was barely audible. "Rachel, I can't trust anybody here. I'm alone." She paused. "And I'm frightened."

Rachel considered. "Victoria, listen to me. Victoria, are you there?"

"Yes."

"Then take a deep breath, be calm, and listen to me just for a moment." Now Rachel's voice was quavering. "You are not alone. I know you need Paladin. I wish I knew where he was, but I don't. I haven't even heard from him for days." There was disappointment in her voice.

"That's because his emails were being intercepted," said Toria.

Rachel paused. "That explains a lot." When Rachel spoke again, her voice was clearer. "All right, for the moment, neither of us have Paladin. But right now you've got me. And you've got to know that you've always got your Heavenly Father. God didn't send Paladin halfway around the world after you to leave you stranded there."

Toria was silent for a moment before she said quietly, "I know."

"Do you?"

"Yes."

"That's my girl," Rachel reassured her. "You've been on your own enough to know how to take care of yourself. Do the best you can, and then just let God make up the difference. Now, when was the last contact you had with Paladin?"

"Sunday," answered Toria. "He wrote me a note—gave me some instructions."

"Then do whatever he said," Rachel directed. "And Victoria, don't be afraid. Everything will work out."

There was another long pause over the line. Finally Toria spoke. "You're a lot like Paladin, aren't you, Rachel?"

Rachel laughed softly. "No, not really. We're kindred spirits, and we're cut from the same cloth. But there's not anybody like Paladin. You know that?"

"Yeah," sighed Toria. She was herself again now. Rachel's

strength, from six thousand miles away, had braced her up and given her courage.

"Meanwhile, Victoria," counseled Rachel, "stay in the embassy. Then no matter what happens in Crimea, at least you'll be safe."

"I wish I could," explained Toria. "I have to go the Royal Palace tonight. Big diplomatic event. I'll be all right, though. Thank you for talking to me. I feel better now. Things *will* be fine, won't they?"

This time it was Rachel who waited to answer. "Yes, they will." After a moment, she added, "Oh, and Victoria—you'll see Paladin again. When you do, would you tell him—I love him?"

Toria paused. "Yes, I'll tell him that from you—with all my heart. Good-bye."

A click over the line signaled that the call was over. Only the dial tone remained.

—

Rachel hung up and turned to Harold Smith, who had been listening to the entire conversation on a nearby extension phone.

He put the receiver down as Rachel came silently over to him, looked up at him, and then buried her face in his shoulder. The old man placed his arms gingerly around her and held her as she silently cried.

"That was hard, wasn't it, my brave girl?"

She said nothing but nodded her head as she sobbed.

"You are a choice young woman, Rachel. I know how sick with worry you are. Yet you chose to build that girl up, because she needed it."

Rachel lifted her face and wiped her tears. "I hope so, Dad. Because I'm afraid for her—and for Paladin, wherever he is. I'm afraid for both of them."

# 16

# MIRACLE AMID THE MUSIC

**O**N TUESDAY MORNING, the Royal Palace of Prince Peter came to life like a beehive. Landscapers meticulously manicured the lawns and gardens. Bakers and cooks busily slaved in the kitchens on the most elegant hors d'oeuvres and desserts. Florists and confectioners arrived with deliveries throughout the day. A large dance orchestra was in place and rehearsing by midmorning. Scores of maids scurried about, cleaning draperies, vacuuming carpets, and dusting every inch of every wall. And then a second army of servants took their place, decorating, rearranging, and transforming the grand ballroom into the centerpiece for the prince's "Coronation Ball."

Of course, this kind of celebration was traditional on the eve of Crimea's national holiday and had been in the planning for months. But the magnitude of this year's fête was on a much grander scale than anyone could remember.

The pomp surrounding it was fabulous. The expense was exorbitant. The guest list alone was well over a thousand persons. In

His Majesty's own words, it was to be "the greatest formal ball to ever have been held in the Royal Palace."

Deep in the bowels of the old foundations, where he languished in the dank castle dungeons, even Paladin Smith was aware of the preparations going on a hundred feet above his head. The commotion rumbled distantly through the underground corridors leading to his cell, though he did not concern himself much with what he heard.

Since yesterday, his guard had dutifully brought him food at meal times, per the colonel's orders. It wasn't much, considering he was in the palace. But it was impressive considering he was in prison. Still, no amount of philosophizing could really persuade Paladin to look at it as more than just food.

So, when the guard brought breakfast to Paladin on Tuesday, it was an easy decision to turn it away and begin a fast. Especially under the realization of how truly desperate his situation was.

He was incarcerated in a foreign country on the verge of chaos, and no American agency knew where he was. He could spend the rest of his life in prison, or in twenty-four hours he could be dead. Under the current circumstances, there weren't a lot of pleasant options. Paladin spent the day in prayer.

At midday, when the guard brought his "lunch"—which looked suspiciously like his reheated breakfast—Paladin politely declined. He did ask for two favors instead. The first was a bucket of clean water and a razor.

"Would you like a towel with that?" asked the guard, stone-faced.

*He must be joking*, thought Paladin but decided not to press his luck. "Oh, you're just too good to me."

"Don't count on it," said the guard and disappeared down the corridor.

Paladin was surprised an hour later when the guard arrived at his cell door with not only the bucket, the razor, *and* a small rough towel, but also with a tiny, used bar of soap floating in the water.

The guard set it down, closed the door, and turned to go when Paladin made his second request.

"Could you get me one other thing? It's very important." The guard froze with his back to the cell. Paladin continued. "Could you please bring me my scriptures—two books in a leather bundle. They're in the briefcase that was brought to the palace with me. Please."

The guard didn't answer but began to walk down the corridor again until he vanished from sight. Fifteen minutes later he returned, unlocked the grate door, and stepped inside, holding Paladin's scriptures and a small candle. He handed them to Paladin and stood silent for a moment. "Are you through with your water?"

"Water? Oh, the water. Yes, thank you. Thank you very much." Paladin handed him the bucket and the towel.

The guard nodded. "I don't suppose you'll want dinner."

"No. No, thank you. I'm fine."

The guard stood again in silence. "Then . . . I'll say my good-byes." He paused, bowed his head slightly, backed out of the cell, and shut the grate with a clang.

Paladin didn't watch him leave this time, but he heard his footsteps grow faint as the guard exited the corridor.

He wasn't sure he liked the feel of that conversation. It sounded so final. It suddenly occurred to him that he'd inadvertently made his "last request" to the warden on duty.

"That's unfortunate. No wonder I hate good-byes," he mumbled to himself as he felt the scriptures in his hand.

He unzipped them and sat on the edge of his cot to read. *I know one thing*, he thought as he steadied the candle on the edge of the wooden frame. *My briefcase isn't far away. Probably in the guardroom since he came back with the books so quickly. Of course, that does me no good if all my stuff is there and I'm here.*

Paladin opened his New Testament to the four Gospels and

began to read at random. Only then did he realize how agitated he truly was. For, in spite of all his bravado, he could not relax—he could not concentrate.

"Why should that be surprising?" he asked, standing up from the cot. "After all, I am very likely going to die."

He shivered and began to breathe deeply. "No," he rebelled against the thought. "I didn't come all this way to end my life in a dungeon. Please, Father, somehow—deliver me from this place. Thou hast not brought me to Crimea to be forgotten here. Not now. Not after so much."

Paladin fell to his knees and listened to his heart in the flickering candlelight. Darkness and silence. He remained there for a long while pondering, searching in the dank quiet for the voice of God. He did not know how long he remained on the floor with his eyes tightly shut. No sound from the palace overhead seemed to pierce his concentration. Nevertheless, no answer to his prayer came to ease his mind. The heavens were closed.

At length Paladin opened his eyes. The small candle still burned on the edge of the cot. He stood and sat on the cold leather straps. Picking up his scriptures, he opened them to read. If he sought the voice of God, it would be found here. He turned to John 14—the narrative of the Savior's final hours. It seemed appropriate to him. Paladin read the first verse.

"Let not your heart be troubled . . ."

Paladin stared at the words. He smiled and breathed deeply of the inspiration that filled and calmed him. He didn't need to breach the veil. The Savior had done it for him long ago. Here were the whisperings of the Spirit. The scriptures were his line of communication to the infinite.

"I am the way, the truth, and the life: no man cometh unto the Father, but by me."

Every word Paladin read was filled with a multitude of meanings. On one level Jesus Christ was bidding farewell and strengthening his disciples. Yet on another, the Savior was speaking to Paladin, strengthening him in an intimate and personal way.

"I will not leave you comfortless: I will come to you."

Paladin read slowly, without hurry, as directed by the Spirit. Each verse was part of a conversation he was carrying on with his Father in Heaven—the most profound revelation he had ever experienced. And yet it was nothing more than the simplest expression of sincere prayer and pure pondering of the sacred word.

"Peace I leave with you, my peace I give unto you; not as the world giveth, give I unto you. Let not your heart be troubled, neither let it be afraid."

Tears filled his eyes as he noted a cross reference in the margin of that verse in his own printing—Matthew 11:28. He knew it well and turned to it.

"Come unto me, all ye that labor and are heavy laden, and I will give you rest."

Come unto me. He had. He would continue to do so. That invitation was his hope, his salvation, his link of survival between life and death. He was heavy laden. So had others been—others much greater than he. Paladin had no right to complain, nor reason to doubt. The Lord would come to his rescue. He always had thus far. And if not . . . all would still be well.

*Rest.* Paladin was beginning to grow very tired. Only then did he realize the flicker of the candle struggling for life on the edge of the cot. Candle wax dripped down the wood frame, forming a small mound on the stone floor, and the wick drooped lazily on its side, ready to expire. Paladin watched it take its last gasp for breath as it extinguished itself and plunged the cell into complete darkness again. But Paladin's world was full of light. He wrapped his scarf around his neck, pulled the blanket up over him, lay down, and slept.

—

Paladin was awakened by music that carried through the passage-ways of the palace to the dungeons below. He opened his eyes and sat up without the disorientation that had overwhelmed him before.

How long had he slept? He glanced at his watch. The display face seemed to illuminate the darkest corners of the cell. It read 11:15 p.m. Paladin had slept through the entire afternoon and into the evening, but he felt refreshed. He was, however, hungry. He'd fasted for the whole day too.

He listened intently to the music. The ball was in full swing. Other events were most likely also unfolding by now. Armies were meeting on the northern border, Crimeans were rioting in the streets, and the world was watching. Paladin stood impatiently. "And I'm stuck here."

*It's time to go.*

"Yes," he answered, running his fingers through his hair. "But there are certain difficulties." He looked around at the stone walls. He was surprised that his eyes were adjusted to the darkness. He could actually see quite passably. But he was still a prisoner.

He was certainly not the first to be cast into prison—Joseph of Egypt, John the Baptist, Joseph Smith—their burdens had been to languish there. Others were likewise taken captive but could not be contained within dungeon walls—Daniel, Alma and Amulek, the Apostle Paul.[10]

*And Peter and John.*

Paladin smiled and thought of Peter and John in the Book of Acts. "But the angel of the Lord by night opened the prison doors, and brought them forth . . ."

Paladin casually stepped to the grate door of the cell and gave it a firm shove. With a gentle click, the door swung open and banged against the wall. Paladin stood, dumbfounded. "It's time to go."

---

10. This list of good men, "persecuted for righteousness sake," includes two Book of Mormon prophets (Alma and Amulek) and Joseph Smith, the founder of The Church of Jesus Christ of Latter-day Saints. Each was unjustly imprisoned in the dungeons of their day for the cause of Christ.

Stepping back to retrieve his scriptures, he stopped only momentarily at the door to look back into the cell. "I'm going to miss this place." Turning, he hurried down the corridor.

Paladin tried to walk as quietly as he could. He made his way along a straight passageway, about two hundred feet long, until he came to an archway and a huge wooden door, which he expected to be locked. He also wasn't sure what was on the other side.

Holding his breath Paladin gripped the handle with both hands and gently pulled. It opened easily. A shaft of light from the adjoining guardroom flooded into the corridor as Paladin peered through the opening.

There in the guardroom, warming by a fire in a tiny stove, sat two guards at a small table. At first Paladin recoiled in fear, for they must have seen him. But then he realized why they hadn't. They were both asleep, sitting in chairs, frozen in place where they had been playing a game of chess to pass the time.

Paladin timidly opened the door, but neither of them stirred. He stood at the entrance, not daring to breathe, and then stepped inside, edging his way to the exit on the other side of the room.

He was halfway there when he glanced to the corridor archway. To his horror, the great wooden door he had left open was slowly beginning to swing closed with an agonizing creak. Paralyzed he watched the huge plank door pick up speed as it groaned on its rusty hinges, finally slamming shut with a reverberating crash that seemed to echo throughout the dungeons.

Paladin had clenched one eye tight while he watched with the other, waiting for the echoes to fade away. When they did, all he could hear were the continued snores of the two guards, still sleeping peacefully in their chairs.

Paladin glanced heavenward and sighed with gratitude. Straightening to his full height, he walked over to the table where the suspended chess game was still in progress. Looking at the board he could see that the guard who had granted his last request was winning. Paladin reached out and took a single knight from the conquered pieces and slipped it into his pocket.

The other guard had apparently just sat down with a late night bowl of borscht from the kitchen—steam still rising from it. The untouched spoon lay beside his hand. The voice of the Spirit whispered, *Eat*. A growl from his stomach confirmed the prompting.

"Excuse me," Paladin said as he took the bowl and sampled a spoonful. It soothed and warmed him from head to toe. "Just like mother used to make."

He lay aside the spoon and drank the soup as he turned to survey the room. Walking over to a cabinet against the wall, he opened it. There, just as he'd hoped, was his briefcase. Setting down the soup bowl, Paladin opened the bag to catalog its contents. He was only looking for a couple of things—his passport and his pouch of American money. Miraculously, it was all there. He supposed he was indebted to the chivalry of Colonel Ustinov for that courtesy.

Paladin quickly stuffed the passport into the pouch and hung it around his neck under his shirt. He wouldn't be needing the briefcase anymore.

Grabbing his scriptures and stepping to the outer door, Paladin took a large set of keys from a peg on the wall and unlocked the large dead bolt. He shoved the huge door open before carefully replacing the keys. Turning to give his jailers one last nod of farewell, he exited the chamber, closing the door behind him.

He found himself in a dark, circular stairwell filled with large stone steps spiraling upward. Paladin remembered being brought down these steps upon arrival at his deluxe accommodations. He ascended them quickly, arriving at another door, beyond which, according to his memory, was a large cellar and then the palace courtyard.

He pushed the door gently open and looked cautiously around. He could hardly expect the Lord to have put the entire castle to sleep. The cellar was empty, but when he listened at the door of the courtyard, he heard passing voices.

Paladin waited, listening to them—a man and a woman—just outside the door. They spoke Russian, which he could not understand. They were also drunk, which he could. He also understood enough from the nuances to know that the gentleman was no gentleman and was up to no good.

This is why Paladin advised his students to avoid lonely courtyards at late night parties. He was even tempted to intercede in the name of the sanctity of womanhood when he heard a quick scuffle, a loud smack, a grunt, and a clamorous crash of metal, followed by retreating feminine footsteps.

Instantly, Paladin yanked open the door and looked around. The courtyard was empty but for the solitary figure of a single individual, collapsed in a heap amongst the ruins of a suit of armor that had stood guard at the cellar door. The man was unconscious. He wore a white tuxedo—and a black eye.

Paladin smiled. He was free. He could hear the music of the ballroom not far away. But that wasn't his concern. He had to get out of here. He stepped over the crumpled figure, taking one last glance at him, and heard a single word echo in his mind.

*Nephi.*

He stopped, considered, and looked at the vanquished drunk again. Wrinkling his brow, he took a deep breath. "Well, you're not quite Laban," he said. "But then again, I don't intend to cut off your head either."[11]

Stooping down, he began to loosen the man's tie.

---

11. In the opening chapters of the Book of Mormon (1 Nephi 3-4), Nephi and his brothers, having fled Jerusalem, are commanded by God to return to Jerusalem to secure the brass plates (the Biblical scriptures) from Laban, a leader of the Jews. In answer to their honest efforts to secure the record, the unscrupulous Laban robs them of their family fortune and attempts to kill them. Led by the Spirit, Nephi returns to Jerusalem by night and discovers Laban collapsed, drunk in the street. Nephi reluctantly obeys the command of the Spirit to behead Laban with his own sword, put on his clothes, and impersonate him at the treasury in order to obtain the sacred record.

It had been a historic night. No one could ever remember a celebration like it. So festive had been the royal ball and so magnificent all the trappings that any hint of crisis on the border or turmoil beyond the palace was all but forgotten in the regal event—an event literally fit for a king.

The prince and the aristocracy who supported him (and who were destined to be rewarded by him) were having a wonderful time. Many of them welcomed the change from the past. Many of them were too stupid to know the difference. All of them lost sight of reality in the gala entertainments while they danced, drank champagne, and ate truffles.

Of course, some of the guests could not forget the pain of what this night signaled to them. Yuri Tiomkin and other high-ranking members of Parliament were obligated to be in attendance. They were invited to personally watch the death of the republic, and it delighted Prince Pyotr to have them present as eyewitnesses to it.

And then there was Ian Keller, who was keenly aware of every detail of the evening's timetable and who did not intend for an instant to forget or ignore a single particular.

As far as he was concerned, all of tonight's events, both inside and outside the palace, were not only orchestrated by him but were also completely under his control. Keller sat on a dais, overlooking the grand ballroom, like Zeus atop Olympus.

From his vantage point he could easily look over the huge hall, which was filled with hundreds and hundreds of guests. Across this sea of Crimea's elite, a red-carpeted, double staircase descended the two opposite walls to the marble dance floor. The polished surface reflected the ballroom's white arched entrances and crystal chandeliers.

Keller glanced carefully at his watch. It was 11:50 p.m. Everything was in place.

So intent was he on his little world that Keller did not at first notice the finger tapping him on the shoulder. He twisted his head, smiling, and looked up. In an instant he turned white. This was a detail he had not anticipated.

"Is this chair taken?" asked Paladin, seating himself comfortably next to Keller. "Please don't make any fuss on my account," he continued. "Let's just talk."

Keller, however, was too confident tonight for such histrionics. He recovered quickly. "You certainly dress up nicely."

"I was hoping you'd recognize me."

"Oh, don't worry," said Keller. "I recognize you, and I know who you are. You're resourceful. But you've overstepped your bounds tonight. You were a fool to come barging in here like this."

Paladin shifted uneasily in his chair. He knew that Keller was absolutely right. But that didn't change the reality of Paladin's world. "Keller, I'm not here because I enjoy your company. I was directed to come and see you."

A puzzled expression momentarily registered on Keller's face. *More riddles from Mr. Paladin Smith,* he thought to himself. *But what are they to me? Why need I have a care in the world for this outcast? This night belongs to me, doesn't it?*

Keller smiled in satisfaction. "Well, actually it's just as well that you're here at this moment that I might enlighten you on the most interesting part of our little chess game—the king and the queen. Notice Prince Pyotr." Keller pointed to the prince across the room.

In regal splendor, Peter stood to the applause of his guests, shining in all his prideful glory. Keller's voice rang with exhilaration. "He is at his zenith. Tomorrow will be his true Coronation Day. But tonight, in just a few moments he will make an announcement that will dazzle his guests. There will be a new crown princess on the throne of Crimea."

This was a detail Paladin had not foreseen. He looked back to the crowd where the prince had just lifted a beautiful young woman by the hand from her chair.

She stood wearing a gown studded with jewels and ribbons, looking every inch a princess. Even across the ballroom she was radiant. At that instant the orchestra struck up a Viennese Waltz, and the crowd edged away to the walls. The prince and his consort stood alone in the center of the ballroom floor.

Pyotr of Crimea bowed gallantly before her and took her in his arms to dance. With her face turned toward him, Paladin beheld perhaps the most beautiful woman he had ever seen—even in her melancholy.

Paladin's face went limp. "Toria!"

"You should have been named for a TV detective," said Keller mockingly, "not a Western gunslinger."

It required all of Paladin's discipline to restrain himself from tearing Keller's head off. "Has Miss Grant been informed of the honor she'll be receiving?"

"A mere trifle. What young woman wouldn't want to be part of a storybook romance? She'll comply. And even if she *is* reluctant, I'm afraid the prince will insist."

"What kind of a medieval world do you live in, Keller?"

"I agree, the drama does have a nice touch. Sorry you won't be here for the wedding, Smith. But by then you'll be dead."

Paladin glanced around the room. As the prince and Toria waltzed, guards on either side of the room inconspicuously made their way to the dais. Keller had gotten their attention.

"Still, I'll always cherish this moment," the ambassador continued, "and I'll always remember how gratifying it was to see that self-satisfied grin wiped off your face."

Standing, Paladin looked at the guards, at the dance floor, and again at Keller. Then gradually the still, small voice he'd come to recognize whispered to him. And as he looked at Keller, a smile slowly crept across his lips.

As it did, Keller's smile disappeared. "Why . . . are you smiling?"

Paladin reached into his pocket, took something out, leaned

down, and held it close for Keller to see. Keller looked at the chess piece from the guardroom table.

"This is the knight," whispered Paladin. "The 'TV gunslinger' you so admire called it the most versatile piece on the chess board. It can move in eight different directions, it can leap over obstacles, and it is always unpredictable. That's what's delightful. God loves surprises." He stuffed the knight into the ambassador's hand. "Checkmate. Good-bye, Keller."

Turning, Paladin stepped off the dais and walked down the short flight of steps onto the ballroom floor.

Keller was speechless, momentarily frozen in place. And without a signal from Keller, the guards themselves stood immobilized, uncertain what to do. The guests around the room also began to whisper in bewilderment as they watched the American envoy step onto the dance floor. This was highly unusual diplomatic behavior. Meanwhile Peter and his consort waltzed, unaware that a lone figure occupied the huge ballroom floor with them—and was on a collision course.

Paladin was aware that almost every eye in the room was on him. He was also aware that he had no idea what he was going to do when he made contact with the prince and Toria. His stomach wrenched in tighter and tighter knots as he neared the middle of the room.

*Lord,* he prayed with all his heart, *you should probably know that I can't dance.*

He continued to walk. They were getting closer. Then he heard the voice in his heart as clearly as he had ever heard any words aloud.

*Don't worry. I dance divinely!*

Paladin blinked with surprise and momentarily broke his stride. But just as quickly he recovered his pace to match the rhythm of the waltz. His timing was perfect. He arrived at the center of the ballroom at the precise moment the Prince had spun Toria to a pause in front of him. The music lapsed into a brief interlude of only seconds as Paladin tapped Peter on the shoulder. "May I cut in?" he asked. The Prince turned and his eyes widened in disbelief.

Paladin didn't wait for an answer. With fluid movement he instantly stepped in front of the Prince and took Toria in his arms. "May I have this dance?" Toria brightened and gazed up at him, too astonished to respond, as the short interlude came to an end. Then, only one thought from the Spirit filled his mind as the waltz resumed.

*Lead with your left.*

He did. Every eye in the room was now focused on them as they danced from the center of the floor in graceful spirals, leaving Prince Peter stunned and alone. Had anyone in the ballroom been watching the prince they would have seen him turn, seething, to catch the eye of Ian Keller. Keller, dumbfounded, stood alone on the dais, helplessly witnessing his chess game spinning out of control.

But no one in the room was watching the prince, enthralled as they were by the performance of the two Americans waltzing on the ballroom floor. And to Paladin and Toria, there were no other people in the room.

Toria studied Paladin's face, speechless, and struggled for words. "Paladin, where have you been?" she asked.

"Not now." Paladin grinned slightly, conscious of his feet moving almost of their own accord.

Toria said nothing, but beamed at Paladin as he scanned the room.

"We've got to get out of here," he said.

"I've got to tell you something first. I promised. It's a message from Rachel." She paused as she looked up into Paladin's face, her eyes glistening. "'I love you.'"

Paladin looked down at her and burst into a smile. "You've talked with Rachel?"

Toria couldn't speak. She simply nodded her head.

At that instant, as the music built to a crescendo, Paladin spun and lifted Toria gracefully into the air in a perfect semicircle, landing her flawlessly on his opposite side.

"Paladin," she spoke, out of breath, "where did you learn to dance?"

"The same place I learned to speak Russian. Now, it's time to go."

Setting Toria's left hand on his right shoulder, Paladin scanned the eyes of the delighted guests. He saw Tiomkin, familiar members of parliament, and other guests he'd met at the reception last week. These were people who could have been his friends—people he would never see again.

Raising his right hand, Paladin smiled and made a broad gesture of invitation. For although he *didn't* know how to dance, he knew instinctively that the audience watching them waltz with such elegance somehow longed to be part of it. He sensed deep inside that this Viennese Waltz was a form of worship, speaking to the soul.

It required no more solicitation than that simple gesture. Immediately men began to bow to the women next to them and stroll to the ballroom floor, or dance out onto the floor from where they stood. By the time Paladin and Toria had circled the ballroom once, the vast expanse was a sea of waltzing forms, flowing in one direction and swirling around the prince, who stood alone at the vortex of this ocean.

—

Coming to himself, Peter struggled angrily to the edge of the room. He shouted for the music to stop, but the final crescendo of the waltz drowned his shrill cries. Only when the orchestra had played the last note and the dancers on the floor had demonstrated their pleasure with a thunderous applause, could the prince's voice begin to be heard.

"Stop! Stop the music!" he shouted. He stood on his toes to search, shoving his way through the crowd. "Where are they? Where are they?"

"Who, your Majesty?" It was Tiomkin who spoke, a polite smile on his face.

The prince was horror struck. "The Americans," he said in quiet confusion before he exploded. "Find them!" he shouted. "FIND THEM!"

# 17

---

# FLIGHT FROM THE PALACE

---

**INDEED PALADIN SMITH** and Victoria Grant were gone—disappeared into the magic of the Viennese Waltz. The joyful abandon of the dance and the pandemonium which followed it had, for the moment, created a perfect setting for their escape.

At the precise moment that the hysterical prince was plunging the celebration into chaos, the two Americans were ascending a staircase in the palace proper which led to the imposing third floor and the imperial quarters designated for the royal family. An alarm began to ring out as they reached the landing.

"This way," shouted Toria as she led Paladin down a long hallway. Hearing the running of footsteps, they hid in a doorway alcove moments before several guards rushed past the end of the corridor fifty feet away. "It's over here," she whispered above the alarm and dashed to a door across the hall, pushing it open.

Toria went immediately to the tiny walk-in closet while Paladin softly shut the door.

The room was elegant and well furnished but modestly small

with a single bathroom—and a French window. Wallpaper and drapes framed the window and door. A single cushioned chair and a reading lamp occupied one corner. Beside it stood a tiny table adorned with a half-read paperback book, turned facedown, and an ash tray holding the remains of few crushed cigarettes.

Paladin looked around. "Hardly a bedroom suited for a queen."

"That's not funny," said Toria, from the closet. "Besides, this isn't my room. This room belongs to Natasha, my lady in waiting. *My* suite is down the hallway and around the corner. I suppose that's where all those guards were headed."

Paladin was impressed. "How did you know to plan your escape so carefully?"

Toria emerged from the closet in a modest pantsuit carrying a small traveling bag.

"I did what you told me. 'Prepare to leave. Travel light,'" she paused. "'And have faith.'"

"Clever girl." Paladin held up his scriptures, which he had retrieved en route. "You can see I did the same, though it's going to take a lot of faith from both of us if we're going to get out of this fortress. Here," he said and tossed her the case holding his books. "Let's keep all this stuff together in that bag of yours."

Going to the door he opened it slightly and peered into the hallway.

Toria unzipped her bag and stuffed the scriptures inside. Slowly she closed it again and looked up. "Paladin. Thank you for coming for me."

Paladin turned to her and smiled reassuringly. "Okay, the hall-way's clear," he said softly as he took the bag from her. "Let's go."

Swinging the door open, he took Toria by the hand and hurried with her out into the corridor.

Turning sharply to their left, they halted, suddenly face-to-face with ten guards who had also stopped, momentarily paralyzed in place. They looked at one another in freeze frame for only a split second before the scene exploded into action.

Paladin and Toria sprinted for the nearest retreat, which was the room they had just exited, while the guards instinctively raised their guns and shouted for them to stop. No sooner had Paladin and Toria slammed and bolted the door, then the wood of the door began to splinter with gunfire.

"You said the hallway was clear!" shouted Toria, backing away from the door.

"Could we talk about it later?" Paladin yelled as he bumped into the corner reading table. He looked down, considered, and picked up the matches beside the ashtray.

Across the room the bedroom door reverberated from the pounding of the guards trying to break it open. The thick oak was not likely to give way easily. The door shuddered again.

"Quick," said Paladin, pointing to the one window. "See if that's a way out."

Toria went to the window and opened the French-style shutters. As she did so Paladin ran to the door and struck a match, lighting the bottom of the drape that framed the door.

"What are you doing?" Toria asked with definite concern.

"I'm giving them more to worry about than us when they *do* break that door in." Paladin stood back from the growing flame and looked at Toria. "How do we look out here?"

"There's a drop of about of about forty feet." She looked to the side. "And a small ledge, about twelve inches wide all along the wall." She looked back at him. "It isn't much."

"It'll have to do." Paladin glanced back at the shuddering door, surrounded now by flames. "Our choices are limited. Here," he said, stepping past her onto the windowsill. "Let me go first."

They both took one last look at the mounting conflagration behind them in the room. Toria sighed. "It was such a nice palace."

Once he was outside, Paladin stepped from the windowsill onto the ledge, which was little more than a narrow decorative cornice that stretched around the outside of the palace just below the level of the third floor windows. It ran to the end of the wall and disappeared around the corner.

Paladin put his weight onto it tentatively, unsure that it would hold him. It was solid enough. The problem was that Paladin could barely fit his foot on the narrow shelf.

He stepped back onto the sill. He was definitely more comfortable with his back against the wall. But that gave them no means of using their hands—and made them totally dependent on balance. One slip and . . .

The pounding at the door was getting louder. There was no time to experiment. Paladin examined the wall quickly and then spoke just loud enough for Toria to hear. "Toria," he said, stepping onto the ledge facing the wall and sinking his fingers into the mortared crevices between the limestone. "Stand here against the masonry, facing the wall as flat as you can. Wedge your fingers between the stones and hold on for life. Come on." He held out his hand.

Toria vanished for an instant and then reappeared, pushing the travel bag out on the windowsill ahead of her.

"No," said Paladin. "Toria, we can't take that. Leave it."

Toria looked at him with determination. "I'm not leaving this behind. I can't."

"What are you talking about?"

"This is important, Paladin."

Without further comment she set the bag precariously on the ledge. "I'll push it with my feet."

Paladin sighed with frustration as she shoved the bag as far along the shelf as she could. Then, taking a deep breath, Toria stepped down onto the cornice. She didn't look below her as she reached the fingers of her left hand up into the crevices between the stones in the wall and tightened her hold into an uncertain grip. With the other hand she closed the remaining French shutter over the bedroom window, quickly repositioning her free hand for another grip in the palace wall.

No sooner had she done so than a tremendous crash was heard inside the room, followed by a clamor of screams and confusion. The guards had finally broken the door in, only to find themselves surrounded by flames.

Their first reaction was, naturally, shock. The second would be self-preservation. But when the panic subsided it would probably occur to them to extinguish the fire and save the palace. All of that gave Paladin and Toria a certain amount of time—but not much—before the guards would resume their pursuit again. Paladin and Toria had to move quickly.

And moving quickly under the circumstances was something they found very difficult to do.

Within seconds a fire siren began to blare through the palace to join the blast of the general alarm. The clock had begun ticking.

A stiff breeze chilled them from the east. Toria glanced up to see clouds overhead. There was a storm in the air. She trembled.

"Don't look down," advised Paladin. "Just move a few inches at a time. We've got to get around the corner before they look through the window."

"All right," answered Toria, shivering with the cold.

Paladin moved slightly away from Toria and saw her squint at the ground below. "Don't look down," he pleaded.

Toria nodded and grit her teeth as she loosened her left grip, and slid her hand inches to her left before clutching another crevice and moving. She glanced at the bag on the shelf between the two of them. Paladin watched as her gaze shifted irresistibly to the palace fountains forty feet below. She clenched her eyes shut.

"Toria," encouraged Paladin.

"I'm okay," she answered as she moved her foot ever so slowly to her left until it touched the bag and nudged it a few inches in Paladin's direction. Sliding it as far as she could, she repositioned her right hand on the wall, before finally bringing her right foot to join the rest of her. She took a long sigh of relief and clung to the wall as if she had just completed a long journey, although she had in reality only moved seven inches along the wall.

Paladin watched and waited wordlessly as Toria opened her eyes and looked at him in the cold and darkness. "I can do this now, Paladin."

Paladin smiled. "I know."

Toria pulled herself up straight. "Well, then, let's go."

Paladin cleared his throat. "Right."

Within a few minutes they had moved almost twenty feet to the end of the palace wall. The only real tricky part was negotiating Toria's traveling bag around the corner of the royal residence. It took both of them and some fancy footwork to do so.

In the process, Paladin was tempted to press her about the necessity of bringing the bag and its precious contents. But he decided not to risk any distraction that would take their minds off the current challenge

As they rounded the corner the noise of sirens faded in the breeze. They were on the south side of the palace now. Below them was a terrace garden that jutted from a reception hall on the second floor.

"It's only a thirty foot drop from here," reassured Toria, "but the fall will still kill you."

"That's comforting," whispered Paladin. "But I think I'll pass. You and I are headed for that balcony over there instead."

Just ahead of them, perhaps twenty-five feet away, a balcony extended from the third floor. Like a welcome port in a storm, it was the haven both of them had worked for—out of the cold, down from the wall, off the ledge. Gratefully they continued to inch forward.

Just then they heard harsh voices in the night. The clipped footsteps of palace guards echoed from the terrace below and stopped just under them. Paladin and Toria both flattened themselves against the stonework wall, and froze.

"You!" Paladin heard a voice bark out in Russian from beneath. He looked to Toria, who stared at him with dread and then shut her eyes.

"You! Wait here and stand watch," barked a squad leader. "The rest of you come with me."

Toria opened her eyes as the footsteps faded into the palace. "It's okay," she mouthed to Paladin and closed her eyes again in relief.

Looking down, Paladin could see a lone guard, already restless with boredom, pacing the garden terrace and lighting a cigarette to warm him in the chill of the night.

Meanwhile, the balcony was almost within reach. Taking a deep breath Toria began to nudge the small bag with her left foot. But as she did so, an uneven joint in the cornice caught at the knob foot of the bag. It turned askew and teetered on the rounded edge of the shelf. With a silent gasp, she reached out to grab it with her left hand, losing her grip with her right as she did so.

Paladin lunged out and grasped her right hand as she stumbled off the shelf toward him, losing his own footing on the ledge as he did so. His left hand flailed wildly at the wall as he was jerked sideways, his fingers just brushing over a rain pipe. Paladin clutched desperately onto it as he slid on top of the ledge, all the while still holding onto Toria with his right hand.

He sprawled there, dazed for an instant, reestablishing his grip on the rain pipe before looking down. At the end of his outstretched arm, clinging to his hand with her fingers, hung Toria. She dangled, struggling silently in midair like a rag doll.

Thirty feet directly below her on the garden terrace stood the palace guard on sentry duty, smoking his cigarette and trying to stay warm. Only the wind had muffled the sound of their struggle from his ears.

"Give me your other hand," Paladin gasped in agony, hardly above a whisper.

Toria winced in pain and looked down. Then Paladin saw it. Suspended from the ends of Toria's fingers hung the troublesome travel bag, about to slip from her grasp to the feet of the oblivious guard. If the bag fell, it would give them away. But what would that matter if he lost his grip on Toria? And right now, both of his hands were losing their strength.

"Please, Toria," Paladin struggled breathlessly. "Forget the bag. Give me your other hand."

Toria jerked her head up at him and gritted her teeth in an anguish of pain and decision.

———

On the terrace below, the guard had just taken a last puff of his cigarette and flicked it into the flower garden. He began to pace away when he heard something hit the ground behind him.

Automatically he spun, drew his rifle, and aimed in the direction of the sound, but he saw no further movement. He straightened cautiously and took out his flashlight, advancing carefully to the wall until the beam of his lantern fell on a small bag lying on its side on the pavement.

He studied it curiously for a moment and then whipped his flashlight into the air as he raised his gun. The wide circle of the beam shone brilliant on the ledge above—but there was no one there. He lowered his rifle, slung it over his shoulder, and shrugged—turning his attention back to the bag.

He stooped down and unzipped it to examine its contents. He took out a set of scriptures in a carrying case and a weathered copy of the Book of Mormon. He found neither very interesting and tossed them aside.

Rummaging inside with his light, he drew forth a wad of women's clothes and lingerie in his fat hands. He fondled through these momentarily and dropped them on the ground. Finally, he nodded with satisfaction as he pulled out a United

States passport and opened it. He recognized the picture of Victoria Grant.

"Umm-hmm," he grunted, picked up the bag, and turned.

"I'll take that," said Paladin, who stood facing the guard, punching him squarely in the jaw.

—

Two realities were immediately apparent to Paladin. The first was how much it hurt his knuckles to hit a man in the face. The second, more gripping reality was that the guard didn't topple before Paladin's crushing blow, but after wincing and turning away, straightened to his full height and smiled.

This was all the more disillusioning in light of reality number three—that the guard was several times larger than he had seemed to be from the ledge or appeared to be as he crouched over the travel bag.

Grabbing Paladin by the collar, the huge guard jerked him around in the direction of the palace, and struck him full in the face with a fist that was like iron.

Paladin fell against the wall but remained standing, though shaken. He rubbed his eyes with his hand, but when his vision cleared all he saw was another fist at close range, smashing into his cheek.

This time Paladin tumbled further along the wall. Struggling to stand upright, he stumbled, catching only dizzying glimpses of the advancing guard. Losing his balance he dropped to the ground but instantly felt a powerful set of fingers grab his shoulder, yanking him upright and turning him, while the guard's other hand reeled back into a fist for a final punch.

Paladin was too dazed to repel the deathblow. Instead he closed one eye while the other remained open as a solitary witness of the impending knockout strike.

Suddenly an explosion of pottery, soil, and flowers shattered on the head of the guard, and he collapsed in a heap at Paladin's feet, like a marionette without strings.

Paladin shook the dirt from his face and fell awkwardly to one knee as he stretched his hands out on the pavement to steady himself. Wiping the soil from his eyes, he strained them open and looked up.

Toria stood on the balcony overhead, holding another flower-pot as her second round of ammunition. "I hated to interfere. You were doing so well."

Paladin wasn't in the mood to respond. "Just climb down here by the trellis on the other side of the balcony—the one I used—and let's get going." She disappeared beyond the railing as he staggered back to the bag and gathered up the debris that had been its contents. "This stuff better be worth it."

—

A door slowly opened into a corridor on the second floor. Paladin cautiously poked his head out and stopped. "All right," he resigned, "then you come and look."

A moment later, Toria's head emerged, scanning the hallway. "All I said was, 'Be more careful this time.'" She walked out into the corridor. "I think you're feeling a little defensive."

Paladin, still a little wobbly, followed her, carrying the travel bag. "I beg your pardon. I'm feeling a little beat up—and slightly lost. Do you know where we are?"

Toria had almost reached the end of the corridor. He took her arm to stop her. "Wait a minute!"

They froze in place and listened. Amid the ringing alarm bell and the blaring of the fire siren, they heard voices and the sound of heavy footsteps—not the frantic running of palace guards but the measured cadence of soldiers boots—coming toward them around the corner.

"Quick," Paladin breathed as they flattened themselves against the wall.

An instant later, a dozen soldiers, dressed in battle fatigues, walked briskly past them and on down the hall, without the least indication that they were looking for them. They remained undetected.

"Those guys seem to know where they're going," considered Paladin. "Is that good enough for you?"

He looked at Toria, and she nodded. Waiting until the soldiers had turned the next corner, Paladin and Toria followed the Spirit—and the soldiers.

Staying on the heels of the Crimean soldiers, without getting too close, was a new and delicate trick in their flight from the palace. Paladin didn't dare leave too much space between himself and his unwitting guides to freedom.

The halls were still teeming with guards and servants, who had to be regularly avoided, placing his lifeline with the soldiers in jeopardy. However, more often than not, the Crimean military conscripts served to clear the way through the palace.

At least twice, a contingent of guards rounded a corner to see the commanding presence of the soldiers coming toward them. In both instances the soldiers not only blocked Paladin and Toria from the guards' sight, but also sent the detail of men scurrying in another direction.

The elite Palace Guard seemed ill at ease in making contact with Colonel Ustinov's highly trained Crimean Military.

The second scattering of the guards was almost disastrous. In the delay that followed, Paladin and Toria almost lost their safe passage, but they finally caught up with the soldiers just as they descended a long flight of stairs and disappeared through a set of double doors at the end of a hallway.

The twists and turns of the palace had finally brought them to an exit, beyond which Paladin heard the noise of vehicles. He and Toria crept up to the doors and opened them a slit to feel the rush of the cold night air.

The soldiers had guided them to the small military compound attached to the palace. Paladin was surprised to find that it had begun to rain outside.

Out in the open enclosure, several soldiers in rain gear were readying trucks and jeeps. Others stood sentinel over the area. And at the far end of the compound was a guardhouse before an impregnable gate.

Paladin's heart sunk. He had brought them to the most highly fortified exit of the entire Royal Palace.

Toria was thinking exactly the same thing. "What have we done?"

Paladin looked to her and smiled. *Of course,* he thought. "We've come to the one spot in the palace where no one would ever expect us to come. And we're going to leave through that gate."

Closing the doors Paladin stood to his full height and looked around. There were small doors off to the side of both walls in the passageway. He tried one that was locked and another that was empty. But behind the third he found what he'd hoped to find—a room lined with pegs for rain slickers and boots.

Paladin pulled Toria inside and quickly sized her up with a raincoat. "Here, put this on and look around for a pair of boots that fit. Maybe they won't recognize us."

Grabbing a rain cap, he crushed it onto her head.

She stopped in mock anger. "Look what you've done to my hair."

"Nonsense," he said, smiling, "you look lovely. Let me see if there's anything here my size."

Seconds later they stood at the double doors again, dressed in rain gear and boots. Their appearance was a stark contrast to that of the soldiers who had preceded them only moments before. No palace guard would have been terrified at the sight of them.

"Okay," assured Paladin, "we don't exactly match the picture of the hardened Crimean regular. Just stay with me, keep your head down, and move quickly."

"It will be interesting watching you requisition one of those trucks."

"Maybe I don't want a truck," said Paladin, peering one last time through the crack in the doors. "But I think I see something that would meet our needs. Let's go."

Swinging the door open, he and Toria stepped into the rainy compound and descended a short flight of concrete steps.

The compound itself was approximately one hundred feet by one hundred feet and was completely enclosed by a high stone barrier—one side of which was the west wall of the palace.

Parked against that wall were several vehicles ready for use at a moment's call. Though soaked and spotted with puddles, the compound was clean and orderly—a mark of palace etiquette and army discipline.

The soldiers assigned to the compound moved about in the rain performing a variety of chores. But they paid practically no attention to the alarms that blared in the palace. At any rate they were too occupied with the heavy shower and their duties to notice two more soldiers entering the enclosure.

At the bottom of the steps stood a fifty-gallon drum sheltered from the rain by an overhang. Atop it lay a clipboard with papers fluttering in a light breeze.

As Paladin passed by, he took the clipboard and began to file through its pages. Very official.

Toria walked smartly beside him as they moved to the edge of the palace wall. A soldier approached on their left, but passed them and kept walking without a glance. *Good*, thought Paladin. *No eye contact. No salutes. Just keep walking.*

And they kept walking, passing truck after truck. "What are we waiting for?" urged Toria under her breath. "Choose a truck and let's go."

"Shh!" Paladin calmed her. "I told you, we're not looking for a truck."

They were nearing the end of the line of vehicles now. There was one more truck—and then a single car.

At that moment a sergeant appeared from the other side of the truck. Standing there like a barrier, he pointed at them and shouted. They froze like statues in mingled dread and confusion. But the sergeant didn't repeat himself or stare them down. This was the army. Expecting to be obeyed, he walked past them to the palace wall, where an open crate revealed hundreds of large cartridge shells.

He shouted again. This time his order was clear enough that Paladin did not need Toria to translate it for him. The sergeant hefted an armload of the shells and carried them to the rear of the nearest truck. They were to follow.

Paladin quickly loaded Toria's arms with as many shells as she could carry and then gathered several himself, hurrying to follow the sergeant to the truck bed where other soldiers were packing the shells inside. A captain was standing at the back of the truck, supervising the operation.

It wasn't until Paladin got close that he recognized him. It was Ustinov's driver—the Crimean captain with piercing eyes who had chauffeured him to the colonel's home a few days before.

Paladin kept his head low, ostensibly intent on his work, quickly returning to the crate to carry more—and hoping the captain didn't notice him or his fellow laborer.

More soldiers joined in the task. Within a few trips, the job was done. Paladin was unsure if those piercing eyes had seen through him.

On his last load to the rear of the truck, Paladin noticed that the captain was gone. He breathed more easily as the soldiers returned to their other duties in the compound, and he met Toria back at the wall.

"That was scary!" she said. Her voice was unsteady.

"It's time to go," he said. "Nobody's watching now. Get into this car." Paladin pointed to the last vehicle—a Mercedes.

Without speaking, they both climbed into the car, closing the perfectly crafted doors with two solid thuds, extinguishing all noise from outside.

"This is the Iron Colonel's car," Toria said in amazement.

"Yes, I've always wanted to drive a limited-edition Mercedes. Quick, check out the glove box, while I look over here."

Toria flipped a latch, and the compartment fell open. "Ugh!" she recoiled. "I found a gun. Is that what I'm looking for?" She closed it.

Paladin fumbled at the dash and steering column in the darkness. "No, we're looking for the keys to the car. Without them this is going to be a very short trip."

Pulling down the sun visor over his head, a set of keys fell into his lap.

"Oh, thank you, Father."

Paladin slipped the key into the ignition and the engine purred to life. Then, turning on the windshield wipers, he slowly backed the car out and shifted the transmission into drive. The enclosure gate stood black in the night ahead of them, fifty feet away.

Toria's voice was earnest. "I don't think you'll find the keys to that so easily."

Pointing the car toward the exit, Paladin inched forward. The sentry at the gate stood at the approach of the vehicle and bared his rifle, a signal for the car to stop.

"Now," said Paladin as he gently applied the brake, "I need you to teach me some Russian."

—

The car rolled to a stop, and the sentry approached the driver with a slightly perplexed look on his face.

"What are you doing with this vehicle?" he called through the rain.

The tinted window rolled down an inch or two.

"The colonel wants his car," responded a man's voice from within—in passable Russian.

"At the front?" quizzed the sentry. "Roll down your window. I'll need to see some authorization."

He waited. There was no acknowledgment, only silence and the rain. He squinted his eyes to identify the unseen individuals in the car through the opening in the window. Something wasn't right.

In one fluid movement the sentry stepped quickly back and pointed his rifle at the driver. Another sentry on the opposite side instantly took aim at the passenger side.

"You will roll down your window, sir."

After a painful pause, the window lowered. The driver stared up into the face of the soldier. The sentry was tense as he continued. "No one drives *this* car."

He shifted his stance and gestured with the rifle. "Please step out, both of you."

Suddenly a hand fell onto the sentry's shoulder. The Crimean captain, the inactive Mormon with the piercing eyes and a knowledge of grammar-school English, stood there in the rain. A distant roll of thunder filled the void as he leaned down and looked intently at the driver through the darkness.

The captain's eyes narrowed in recognition. Raindrops pattered relentlessly on the open window and splashed into the car. He looked from Paladin to Toria and back to Paladin again for a few moments before his gaze drifted past them—to nowhere in particular.

At length, the captain fixed his eyes on the American again and straightened to his full height.

"Corporal," he said and inhaled deeply, "this man is authorized."

"But, Captain . . . ," the sentry objected as he continued to level his gun.

"Open the gate and see him through," the captain ordered. "The colonel wants his car." He still had not taken his eyes from Paladin.

"Yes, sir."

Paladin watched as the corporal reluctantly shouldered his rifle and nodded to the other sentry. They both retreated to the guard-house, and within seconds the gate clanked open.

The wipers continued to splash the falling rain from the wind-shield. Paladin looked into the captain's piercing eyes.

"*Spacibo*," Toria said quietly in the shadows.

The captain maintained his stare and merely nodded, without smile or explanation, as he passed them through the gate with a gesture of his hand.

Paladin raised the window, shifted the car into first gear, and drove through the granite opening that led from the palace compound. He glanced through the rearview mirror to see the captain still looking at him as the gate to the compound closed between them.

Toria spoke very softly. "Paladin, who was that?"

When he answered, Paladin's voice was quiet. "One of the angels of heaven."

# 18

# The Battle of Coronation Day

T HE CLOCK ON the dash read 2:45 a.m. It amazed Paladin to realize how long it had taken them to escape from the palace. He was also surprised at the level of activity in Rostov at this time of morning.

Cars clogged the streets, honking horns at people who overflowed from the sidewalks. Clumps of humanity crowded around bonfires for warmth—and camaraderie. Other throngs listened to speeches or chanted and carried posters. Signs and placards were everywhere. They hung over streets, on walls, and outside windows. The city was in turmoil.

"Is this typical Coronation Day behavior in Rostov?" asked Paladin.

Toria responded with surprise. "You have no idea what's happened since you were arrested, do you?"

"No, Toria, you don't get a lot of news in the palace dungeons. The colonel did tell me the people were upset."

"Paladin, Crimea is near riot. You spoke to the archbishop,

196

and he spoke to them. This is the result. They're ready to boil over. We're looking at revolution when the Russians cross the border."

At that instant a group of shouting students ran in front of the car. Paladin slammed on the brakes.

"Well, we've got to get out of this. Tell me which way to go."

"Head east as soon as you can," suggested Toria. "That's the quickest way back to the embassy."

Paladin stopped behind a line of cars. "Toria, I don't think we should go to the embassy."

Toria turned to look at him in shock. "Paladin, the country is at war and in riot. Persona non grata or not, the embassy's got to give you sanctuary – in spite of Keller."

"I'm not worried about my badge of dishonor," said Paladin. "And as for Keller, I don't think he'll be going back to the embassy."

"Then what are we arguing about," countered Toria. The embassy is the safest place for us now."

"Toria," Paladin reasoned, "we don't belong in the safest place. That's not our purpose here. As we speak, Crimea is being invaded."

"But, Paladin, what can we do about it? We're just two people. How can we stop the rockets and the tanks or the people fighting in the streets? If we don't get back to the embassy now, we may never get back."

"So we have a choice," said Paladin calmly. "We can watch this country crumble from the windows of the American Embassy—or we can make a difference fighting in the streets. What will it be?"

Toria looked into the darkness of the night. All around them the fires continued to burn on corners, and the shouting echoed in the streets. She sat back, overwhelmed.

"Toria, I promised you at the White Cathedral that I came to help these people. When I made that promise, I didn't know what it meant. I think I've finally figured it out." He paused. "God has something for you and me to do."

Toria slowly turned to look at him.

"You wanted to be part of the solution," Paladin continued. "Now it's time to be part of history."

Paladin watched her face harden with resolve. "Where do we need to go?" Toria asked.

Paladin smiled and proceeded forward again. "Well, I did commit myself to bringing the colonel his Mercedes. But we've got to find him."

"The sentry said he's at the front," said Toria. "Do you really want to drive into a battle?"

"Well, it's the best place to stop an invasion," noted Paladin. "But it's a long border. I knew I should have asked directions at the compound when I had the chance."

"Well, we *are* in the colonel's car," observed Toria. "Can't we radio headquarters or something?"

"I don't think they'd share much." Paladin brightened. "But we could eavesdrop. Here, let's turn this thing on."

Paladin carefully pressed a button next to the radio on the dash. The display instantly lit up into a dazzling array of data as sound and static burst from the ceiling speakers. Several conversations seemed to bombard their ears at once.

"Wow," Paladin shouted as he turned the volume down. "That certainly brought on an information overload. Quick," he listened more intently, "see what you can pick up from all this."

Toria leaned forward and bent her head toward the speaker on the dash to listen to the chatter. Paladin glanced at her and held his breath as she closed her eyes to concentrate. Her profile was illuminated intermittently by the streetlights overhead. After a few minutes, her eyes popped open. She looked at Paladin and smiled.

"What did you get?"

"Well, as near as I can tell the actual invasion begins at dawn—that's about 5:30. The Russian forces and the Crimean army are stretched halfway across the border at strategic points. But the spearhead units are gathering just north of a little berg called Konstantinovskiy. That's where Ustinov is."

"Then that's where we're headed."

"It's about two hours northeast of here," explained Toria.

"Good. Then we'd better get going." Paladin looked around at the highway markers on the street. "Can you show me the way there?"

Toria grinned and tapped the display. "I don't have to. It's on the colonel's GPS."

There on the dash was a clear map through the Crimean foothills north of Rostov to the town of Konstantinovskiy.

Paladin smirked and straightened in his seat. "Well, navigator, point me in the right direction. We've got a lot of ground to cover before the sun comes up."

—

If one were to plan a "non-hostile invasion" of a neighboring country Konstantinovskiy would be the ideal site from which to stage it. Centrally located on the Crimean border, it offers the advantages of unilateral positioning from which to direct and deploy troops. It is also conveniently situated on the Don River just south of Volgograd—providing a stable potential supply line to an established Russian stronghold. Novoshokhtinsk to the west, and forty-nine miles north of Rostov, also features appealing qualities as a competitive spot. But its proximity to the Ukrainian border would create potential international and diplomatic difficulties. So, overall, Konstantinovskiy is the most attractive site available. And it is the rule in military strategy as it is in real estate—location, location, location.

Novoshokhtinsk would also have been a much more convenient destination for Paladin and Toria. As it was, they found themselves driving over one hundred miles through the stark countryside of Crimea in search of two armies—and by anyone's reasoned judgment, into certain death.

"Paladin?" asked Toria, breaking the silence of more than a half hour of driving.

"Are you still awake?" asked Paladin. "You'd been so quiet I thought you'd gone to sleep—or I'd hoped you'd gone to sleep."

"No. I've been thinking."

"Yeah," he echoed, "me too." They were reading each other's thoughts.

"We're going to find Ustinov, right?"

"Right."

"What are we going to do when we find him?"

Paladin sighed. "I haven't the faintest idea."

He glanced over to her again and could see her eyes studying him in the faint glow of the dashboard lights. She wasn't shocked—merely observant.

"Toria, you don't realize that most of this entire week has been like that. From one step to the other I haven't had a clue what's been coming next. The only thing I've known for sure is that the Spirit has been guiding me. It's like the prophets say about walking to the edge of the light and then taking a few steps into the darkness. They promise the light will always follow. And it always has. Now the Spirit has impressed me to go to Konstantinovskiy. And I know the light will follow. It always does."

Toria was silent as she pondered. "That's what they call faith, isn't it? You have faith, Paladin. But I don't know if I do. I'm afraid to die."

"Oh, we're not going to die. Well, you're not anyway. You're too important. You're the reason I've come. The Lord will make sure of that."

Toria was suddenly upset. "Don't talk that way. You're not going to die. You can't."

"Toria, settle down. Believe me, I intend to survive if I have any say in the matter. But so far the Spirit hasn't let me know any details. We'll find out soon enough. For right now, you need to rest a little."

Paladin pulled a light blanket in the front seat over her with his free hand. "And I need to think. Everything will be just fine. You'll see."

Toria was exhausted. She nodded and nestled her head against the cushions of the front seat, closing her eyes. Turning restlessly trying to get comfortable, she finally became still and began breathing more deeply.

Paladin watched her for a long minute, until, sure that she was asleep, he turned his full attention to the road ahead. But in reality he was just as restless and just as distracted as Toria. Of all that he had faced this week, this was his most formidable challenge. What *was* he going to do when he arrived at the front? Just what surprises did the Lord have in store for them?

—

"Toria!" She was up like a skyrocket as she heard her name. The shock of consciousness left her in complete disorientation.

She looked around the car quickly. The interior was dimly illuminated in twilight. In the driver's seat sat Paladin, straight as a guard at attention.

"Toria, we're in trouble. Look at this."

Surveying the countryside around them, Toria instantly saw more than the farmlands and fields of Northern Crimea. Everywhere along the small road they were driving on there were soldiers and vehicles.

"Where are we?" she asked.

"I've been following the GPS. I got off the main highway about a half hour ago and suddenly found myself clogged in the middle of this." Paladin pointed ahead.

On the road in front of them were two trucks filled with soldiers, no doubt on their way to the spearhead point. Behind them there were other trucks and jeeps.

"How could I have been so stupid?" said Paladin.

"Why didn't you wake me earlier?" she asked.

"There was no need until now. We've been moving. But look up there."

Beyond them, up a short hill, the soldiers had set up an inspection point. The first truck was just stopping at it.

"What made me think I could just drive through here? This is an army with picket lines and checkpoints."

The first truck began to move, and the second truck stopped at the soldier's command. Paladin and Toria could see the driver presenting papers.

"We don't have any papers," said Toria.

"We don't have anything but a stolen Mercedes." Paladin sighed, gripping the steering wheel.

"We've got prayer. Paladin, you said the Spirit sent you here. Then ask God to find you a way through."

"Pray, Toria," was all that he could say as the second truck drove through, and the soldier on guard waved Paladin to move forward.

He pressed the accelerator and the car slowly approached the checkpoint where the soldier waited. Toria clenched her eyes shut as Paladin pushed the brakes and almost brought the car to a halt.

Then, in an instant, the soldier's stern expression eased, and instead of halting them, he nodded and waved them through the station. Paladin slowly released his foot off the brake.

The soldier nodded more energetically and continued to wave them through, saluting at the last minute as they passed him.

Paladin looked on the road behind them to see the soldier routinely stopping the next truck to check papers as he had done to all those before.

"Toria, we're through."

She opened her eyes and looked behind as well. "But how?"

"Prayer—and a stolen Mercedes." Paladin closed his eyes quickly to say a prayer of his own. "Praise the Lord. What else would incline the picket to assume that the colonel himself were inside this car?"

—

The colonel's Mercedes encountered two additional checkpoints within the next five miles. At each picket the same prayer was met with the same response and salute as they were waved through.

Soon the trucks ahead of them turned off to the side to join various units, and Paladin and Toria found themselves alone on the convoy road. But as the light of dawn advanced, Paladin saw that they had entered onto a great field of battle and were surrounded by the machinery of war. They had found the armies of "invasion."

It was an eerie sensation to wind through the rolling hills between the fronts of the two forces, poised as twin juggernauts to move forward and smash the liberty of a free people. The Russian tanks and assault vehicles were well marked with banners of red—the trappings of an already victorious army which intended to enter as conquerors and saviors. These were the command units of the advance line. Behind them, already in subservient positions of support, crawled the Crimean army. It was obvious to Paladin how this was playing out.

He shook his head. "What a joke!"

"Shh!" ordered Toria. She had turned up the radio. The chatter was dizzying. "They're talking about us. There's a lot of confusion. The field commanders are asking about our identity. They've concluded that we're not the colonel."

She listened again. "They're challenging now. Demanding we identify ourselves. They want to know what we want."

Paladin considered for a moment and slowed the car to a stop. Then he set the brake and smiled.

"Well," he unlatched the handset from the radio and held it out to her. "I guess it's time to answer a direct question. Tell them we're looking for Colonel Ustinov."

Toria took the handset with uncertainty, pursed her lips, and nodded. She took a breath and pressed the button. "*Mie ishchem Polkovnika Ustinova.*"

The chatter subsided, but there was no response.

"Repeat the message," said Paladin. "And tell them who we are."

Toria exhaled deeply and started again. "*Nashi imena—Paladin Smit I Viktoria Grant. My ischem Polkovnika Ustinova.*" She released the button and waited.

Suddenly a deep clear voice resonated over the radio. Paladin would never mistake that voice. "*Vy nashli yego.*"

"What did he say?"

Toria looked at Paladin and swallowed. "You found him."

"Let me speak to Mr. Smith," said the colonel. It was not a request. Toria gave the handset to Paladin.

"Colonel, please, I've come over a hundred miles to see you."

"Then face forward, Mr. Smith, and look at me. I'm afraid this is as close as we may come under the circumstances."

Paladin had been looking down and sideways at the radio. Slowly he lifted his head and squinted through the exhaust of the preparing vehicles in the cold light of dawn. There in the clearing smoke, seventy-five feet away, hulked a massive tank, on the brow of a hill. They both stared at it for a moment in silence.

"Here," said the colonel, "let me assure you that it is me."

Instantly there was a grinding sound. The turret of the tank slowly swiveled in the direction of the Mercedes, and the massive cannon took direct aim at the front of the car.

"There. This is my way of saying, 'Hello.'"

Toria took the device. "Colonel, please . . ."

"Silence, both of you," he ordered. "You have done something extremely foolish. I thought better of you. Can't you see? Look around you. Things much larger than you or I are happening here. This is the passage of time—the march of nations."

"But you—you can change it," argued Paladin.

"I can change nothing. I clarified my loyalties to you. This is my place."

Another voice came over the radio—a harsh Russian voice. Ustinov responded briefly.

"Do you hear that voice, Mr. Smith? That is the man in charge of this offensive into Crimea. His name is General Leski of the Army of the Russian Federation. Turn around, and let me introduce you to him. You happen to have stopped directly between us."

Paladin turned to look out of the rear windshield. There, one hundred feet behind them crouched an assault vehicle, idling. As he watched, a hatchway opened, and from it stood a commanding-looking individual with hardened features who turned and glared menacingly at the Mercedes. His face was a cold steel expression of heartless will and cruelty. He was the bookend of Colonel Ustinov—but with none of the humanity.

"Take a good look at him," said the Colonel. "In five minutes General Leski will lead the joint armies of Crimea and Russia into a new era. And I will follow him because this is who I am. These are our choices, Mr. Smith. We spoke of yours. This is mine."

"You've told me this before, Colonel. Why repeat yourself? Who are you trying to convince?"

"Enough." The colonel spoke some Russian words, and two soldiers from his line climbed from another vehicle and approached the car.

Toria stiffened. "Paladin!"

Ustinov continued. "These men are coming to place you under arrest and take my car from the field."

Paladin considered quickly, reached over, and popped open the glove box. His right hand gripped the service revolver as he held the radio with his left.

"You know I've got a pistol in here, Colonel. Tell those soldiers to back away."

Momentarily the solders stopped short, confused.

"Very well. If you insist, I will have to take care of you myself."

Paladin watched as the cannon of the tank raised and lowered until the muzzle aimed at the front windshield of the Mercedes.

"Now, step from the car, the both of you."

Toria stirred. Paladin dropped the gun and grabbed her arm.

"I assure you, Mr. Smith," Ustinov continued, "to me it is just a car. And I am determined to demonstrate my commitment to the general. I am a soldier first."

"So," said Paladin, "this is the Iron Colonel. How else can we impress the general?"

"You don't understand," said Ustinov. His voice had changed slightly. "You of the West will never comprehend the commitment of a man to his king."

Paladin glanced behind them again. General Leski stood impatiently, shouting. He yelled down into his vehicle. Suddenly Paladin heard his voice over the radio—uncontrollable and furious.

There was a long pause over the speaker. Ustinov finally spoke. "It is time for this army to move. And for you to make your decision. Live or die."

"We all stand at the crossroads, Colonel." Paladin glanced quickly through the rear windshield.

General Leski convulsed with rage as he screamed incomprehensible orders at the minions around him. Russian soldiers leaped from nearby vehicles, rifles held chest-high, and began running toward the Mercedes. He was no longer waiting for the Colonel to act.

Paladin continued, "It is as you say, sir. I've made my decision. And it's time for you to make yours. That decision has been made by every patriot who ever lived—Jefferson, Adams, Franklin—and George Washington."

Paladin looked at the group of soldiers. They were getting closer. "Ultimately, sir, every great man has to choose between his king—and his country."

Paladin released the button and laid the handset beside him. All was silent on the radio as he and Toria sat, staring down the muzzle of the tank's cannon. Except for the approaching soldiers behind them, the field of battle was totally still.

Then, suddenly the cannon of the tank lowered, pointing at the grill of the car before recalibrating, rising ever so slightly—it seemed to them only a few inches.

"Good-bye, Mr. Smith," were the Colonel's only parting words.

Instantly the cannon fired in a deafening explosion. Flames belched from the muzzle as the shell from the tank shot past the roof of the Mercedes and scored a direct hit on the assault vehicle of General Leski, engulfing it in a ball of fire.

Toria twisted, wide-eyed and screaming, to see the Russian soldiers turn in place and retreat to their lines in confusion. Paladin looked around them in a sweeping panorama. The entire field was a picture of sudden pandemonium.

"Attention all ground and air forces," they heard the colonel's powerful voice over the radio. "A hostile force of Russian troops and artillery has crossed our borders at key northern points. Commanders of all units! Repel the invading army. I repeat, repel the invading army."

As if every soldier and military vehicle had been waiting for this order, the Crimean line instantly erupted into a volley of destruction. Without hesitation, the tanks, other vehicles, and infantry moved forward into commanding positions over their supposedly superior foe.

"Paladin!" shouted Toria. "Get us out of here!"

Paladin didn't need a second invitation. Grinding the idling Mercedes into gear, he gunned the engine into a screaming whine. A torrent of mud and undergrowth spewed from the rear wheels as the car bolted forward, just ahead of the colonel's advancing tank.

Beside them, a shell exploded, followed by another directly in their path, showering the hood and windshield with soil and rocks.

Paladin twisted the wheel violently as the car careened into the armored wall of another tank, which continued to grate past them without a pause.

He shifted gears and shoved his foot to the floor again as they lurched between a gap in the first wave of tanks to narrowly avoid being crushed amid the footsteps of war.

Explosions continued to rain around them as Paladin dodged the fiery blasts and the obstacles of a terrain never intended for a luxury vehicle. Sliding in a bog of mud, the Mercedes spun out of control and reeled into a tree where it momentarily stopped.

Paladin sat up and shook his head. "Toria, are you okay?"

"Yes," said Toria, straightening herself and panting breathlessly. "Are we out of danger?"

Looking around, Paladin strained his eyes to see past the smoke of the battlefield. In the distance, a few hundred feet away, a second wave of Crimean artillery was rapidly approaching. Suddenly another volley of deafening explosions flared around them, covering the car with a layer of dirt. He squinted behind them through the dust and flames to see a platoon of three Russian tanks retreating from the front lines and heading directly toward them.

With a glance at Toria, Paladin rammed the car forward, scraping past the tree as it spun and finally leaped from the mud, away from the Russians—on a collision course with the advancing Crimean army.

"Are you sure about this?" yelled Toria above the exploding shells.

"It's the quickest way out of here!" Paladin shouted back as he shifted into third gear.

With each second they sped faster across the bare landscape. And with each second the Crimean tanks loomed larger. Explosions continued to blast and pock the landscape around them, creating a deadly obstacle course of craters and fire.

Suddenly a mortar burst so near that the car reeled up on two wheels before falling to the solid earth again as Paladin struggled to maintain control. Careening at a full eighty miles per hour, the Mercedes shot through the line of armored vehicles and past the units of infantry who followed them.

In an instant Paladin and Toria found themselves clear of the gauntlet of violence, and bounced, skidding onto a country road. Paladin never slackened his speed as he raced down the dirt path away from the battlefield. Gradually the noise of war faded into the distance behind them.

# 19

# OUTCASTS IN A STRANGE LAND

**D**AWN ON WEDNESDAY found the bulk of the Russian force racing southwest, while defending themselves from the pent-up anger of the Crimean army that pursued them from the rear.

A similar picture was being replayed all across the northern border. Before the morning was over, the Russians would be met by other Crimean divisions anxious to enter the fray from the south to answer the call of their colonel and commander-in-chief.

The "Battle of Coronation Day" would be the greatest rout in the nation's history—the hammer stroke of 600,000 frustrated soldiers in defense of their freedom against an arrogant but unprepared invading army, who had assumed they were going to a parade instead of a war.

Meanwhile, east of the battles, in the central farmlands of Crimea, a solitary, crippled Mercedes raced south through the rolling Caspian hills in an effort to flee the chaos of war.

After their escape from the battlefield of Konstantinovskiy, neither Paladin nor Toria spoke for a long time. Their minds were reverently absorbed in a myriad of images and emotions – quiet reflections radiating in the soft glow of their personal miracle.

Flashes of memory—from this morning and yesterday and the past week—cascaded into Paladin's consciousness, almost overwhelming him.

Yet it had all happened. They had changed history. The freedom of a nation had been preserved and over forty million people were safe and secure in their liberty.

Still, beyond the pastoral farmlands of the countryside, war raged in the nations's interior. Violence and unrest—the labor pains of a reborn democracy—were destined to torture a fragmented populace for several days before order would begin to be restored.

But a quieter reality rested on the two companions speeding through the lowlands of Crimea.

"Thank you, Paladin," Toria finally spoke in a voice barely above a whisper. "Thank you for keeping your promise. You came to rescue me and ended up rescuing Crimea."

Paladin shook his head thoughtfully. "I think it was you who did that."

She took a deep breath and exhaled with a sigh. "Paladin, we've been a part of something wonderful."

"It's hard to believe, isn't it?" he said softly.

Toria smiled. "No, it isn't so hard to believe anything anymore." She swallowed hard and looked at him. "God lives, doesn't He, Paladin?"

Choking back a surge of emotion, Paladin nodded. "Yes, he does."

They sat again in silence as the Spirit enveloped them in warmth and witness. But the Spirit also whispered other truths to their hearts. For the triumph of the morning was but a moment for them. The unspoken power of eternity quietly testified that Crimea was no safe place for them. Like so many impressions Paladin couldn't explain, he knew he was being directed to flee Eastern Europe, and to do so as quickly as possible.

Yet the Spirit also whispered to Paladin and Toria in a voice of power and comfort that filled their souls with peace in the midst of turmoil. They had been blessed to participate in something grand and miraculous. The Lord had allowed them to touch a life or two and change the fate of a nation—and, in that sense, influence the fate of the world.

Paladin didn't understand why he, of all people, had been selected by destiny to be a part of this adventure. Nor did he know what awaited him now that it was all over. And he didn't understand how Victoria Grant fit into the Lord's intriguing puzzle.

All he recognized for certain was what the Spirit now spoke in sacred tones to his soul: *Well done, thou good and faithful servant.* That was enough. And it was enough that he was driving away from danger, from adventure, from intrigue—and headed for home.

**S**TEPHEN J. STIRLING was born in Los Angeles, California, and grew up in Huntington Park in Southeast LA. Graduating from high school in 1970, he received a scholarship to Brigham Young University at the age of seventeen.

He earned a bachelor's degree in journalism in 1976 and spent the next few years wandering America in search of adventure. Interspersed through his college career and days on the road, he served a mission in Chile and taught for eight years as an early morning seminary teacher.

Settling briefly in Chicago, he entered the profession of advertising, a field in which he ultimately held many positions with companies from the Midwest to the Pacific coast. He eventually planted roots in Orange County, California, where he established Stirling Communications and spent fifteen years as a freelance copywriter, scriptwriter, and video producer.

In 1994 he was hired by the Church Educational System and relocated with his family to Gilbert, Arizona, where he has fulfilled a lifelong dream of teaching released-time seminary for the past twenty years.

He and his wife, Diane, were married in 1981 and are the parents of five children—Jennifer, Lindsey, Brooke, Marina, and Vladimir. Brother Stirling is the author of several books, including *The Ultimate Catalogue* and *Shedding Light on the Dark Side*.